ACCLAIM FOR TOBIAS WOLFF

The Night in Question

"Simply lovely. . . . [Wolff's] plots burn with the passion of a storyteller obsessed with what he knows. . . . Tobias Wolff has the heart of a writer, and that is no small treasure."
—*Boston Globe*

"Wolff is among the most gifted of today's writers. . . . [His] work is beautiful and wise . . . both subtle and passionate."
—*Times Literary Supplement* (London)

"Puts us in the hands of a master craftsman. . . . Intricate and highly compressed, Tobias Wolff's explorations of our emotional and moral infrastructures are psychological travelogues. . . . [He] shows us ourselves in all our graceless glory."
—A. M. Homes, *Bomb*

"With a hand light and deft enough for neurosurgery, he takes a common experience . . . and carves from it powerful drama and elemental emotion. . . . [These are] magnificent stories."
—*San Francisco Chronicle*

"Perhaps the most enjoyable American short story writer working today."
—*Cleveland Plain Dealer*

"The best of [these fictions] are certainly among the most accomplished being written in our time."
—*Kirkus Reviews*

TOBIAS WOLFF

The Night in Question

Tobias Wolff's memoir of Vietnam, *In Pharaoh's Army*, was a finalist for the National Book Award, and his childhood memoir, *This Boy's Life*, won the *Los Angeles Times* Book Award in 1989. His other books include two story collections, *In the Garden of North American Martyrs* and *Back in the World*, and *The Barracks Thief*, a short novel for which he received the PEN/Faulkner Award. He has also won the Rea Award for excellence in the short story. He lives with his family in upstate New York, where he is writer-in-residence at Syracuse University. The stories in *The Night in Question*—three of which were selected for the *Best American* series—have appeared in periodicals ranging from *Antaeus* to *The New Yorker*, *Story* to *Granta*, *TriQuarterly* to *Esquire*.

The Night in Question

The Night in Question

STORIES

TOBIAS WOLFF

VINTAGE CONTEMPORARIES

Vintage Books

A Division of Random House, Inc.

New York

The stories in this collection were originally published in the following:

Antaeus: "Migraine" and "Two Boys and a Girl"; *The Atlantic*: "The Other Miller" and "Sanity"; *Doubletake*: "Flyboys"; *Esquire*:"The Chain" and "Smorgasbord"; *Granta*: "Casualty"; *Harper's*: "Lady's Dream"; *The New York Times Magazine*: "Powder"; *The New Yorker*: "Bullet in the Brain" and "The Night in Question"; *Story*: "Firelight"; *TriQuarterly*: "The Life of the Body." "Mortals" was published in *Listening to Ourselves* by Anchor Books, in 1993. "The Other Miller," "Smorgasbord," and "Firelight" were selected for *Best American Short Stories* in 1986, 1987, and 1992, respectively. "The Life of the Body" appeared in the 1991 *Pushcart Prize* volume.

The Library of Congress has cataloged the Knopf edition as follows:
Wolff, Tobias, [date]
The night in question : stories / by Tobias Wolff.—1st ed.
p. cm.
ISBN 0-679-40218-7
1. Manners and customs—Fiction. I. Title.
PS3573.O558N54   1996
813'.54—dc20   96-17560
CIP
Vintage ISBN: 0-679-78155-2

Author photograph © Marion Ettlinger

Random House Web address: http://www.randomhouse.com

Printed in the United States of America
20 19 18 17 16 15

For Mary Elizabeth

For their many valuable readings of these stories over the years, I would like to thank my wife, Catherine, and my editor, Gary Fisketjon. Thanks as well to Amanda Urban, Liz Calder, and Peter Straus.

Finally, I am deeply grateful to the Whiting Foundation, the Lyndhurst Foundation, and the Lila Wallace–Reader's Digest Foundation for their generous encouragement and support.

Contents

The Night in Question

Mortals

The metro editor called my name across the newsroom and beckoned to me. When I got to his office he was behind the desk. A man and a woman were there with him, the man nervous on his feet, the woman in a chair, bony-faced and vigilant, holding the straps of her bag with both hands. Her suit was the same bluish gray as her hair. There was something soldierly about her. The man was short, doughy, rounded off. The burst vessels in his cheeks gave him a merry look until he smiled.

"I didn't want to make a scene," he said. "We just thought you should know." He looked at his wife.

"You bet I should know," the metro editor said. "This is Mr. Givens," he said to me, "Mr. Ronald Givens. Name ring a bell?"

"Vaguely."

"I'll give you a hint. He's not dead."

"Okay," I said. "I've got it."

"Another hint," the metro editor said. Then he read aloud, from that morning's paper, the obituary I had written announcing Mr. Givens's death. I'd written a whole slew of obits the day before, over twenty of them, and I didn't remember much of it, but I did remember the part about him working for the IRS for thirty years. I'd recently had problems with the IRS, so that stuck in my mind.

As Givens listened to his obituary he looked from one to the other of us. He wasn't as short as I'd first thought. It was an impression he created by hunching his shoulders and thrusting his neck forward like a turtle. His eyes were soft, restless. He used them like a peasant, in swift measuring glances with his face averted.

He laughed when the metro editor was through. "Well, it's accurate," he said. "I'll give you that."

"Except for one thing." The woman was staring at me.

"I owe you an apology," I told Givens. "It looks like somebody pulled the wool over my eyes."

"Apology accepted!" Givens said. He rubbed his hands together as if we'd all just signed something. "You have to see the humor, Dolly. What was it Mark Twain said? 'The reports of my death—' "

"So what happened?" the metro editor said to me.

"I wish I knew."

"That's not good enough," the woman said.

"Dolly's pretty upset," Givens said.

"She has every right to be upset," the metro editor said. "Who called in the notice?" he asked me.

"To tell the truth, I don't remember. I suppose it was somebody from the funeral home."

"You call them back?"

"I don't believe I did, no."

"Check with the family?"

"He most certainly did not," Mrs. Givens said.

"No," I said.

The metro editor said, "What do we do before we run an obituary?"

"Check back with the funeral home and the family."

"But you didn't do that."

"No, sir. I guess I didn't."

"Why not?"

I made a helpless gesture with my hands and tried to appear properly stricken, but I had no answer. The truth was, I never followed those procedures. People were dying all the time. I hadn't seen the point in asking their families if they were really dead, or calling funeral parlors back to make sure the funeral parlors had just called me. All this procedural stuff was a waste of time, I'd decided; it didn't seem possible that anyone could amuse himself by concocting phony death notices and impersonating undertakers. Now I saw that this was foolish of me, and showed a radical failure of appreciation for the varieties of human pleasure.

But there was more to it than that. Since I was still on the bottom rung in metro, I wrote a lot of obituaries. Some days they gave me a choice between that and marriage bulletins, but most of the time obits were all I did, one after another, morning to night. After four months of this duty I was full of the consciousness of death. It soured me. It puffed me up with morbid snobbery, the feeling that I knew a secret nobody else had even begun to suspect. It made me wearily philosophical about the value of faith and passion and hard work, at a time when my life required all of these. It got me down.

I should have quit, but I didn't want to go back to the kind of jobs I'd had before a friend's father fixed me up with this one—waiting on tables, mostly, pulling night security in apartment buildings, anything that would leave my days free for writing. I'd lived like this for three years, and what did I have to show for it? A few stories in literary journals that nobody read, including me. I began to lose my nerve. I'd given up a lot for my writing, and it wasn't giving anything back—not respectability, nor money, nor love. So when this job came up I took it. I hated it and did it badly, but I meant to keep it. Someday I'd move over to the police beat. Things would get better.

I was hoping that the metro editor would take his pound of flesh and let me go, but he kept after me with questions, probably showing off for Givens and his wife, letting them see a real newshound at work. In the end I was forced to admit that I hadn't called any other families or funeral homes that day, nor, in actual fact, for a good long time.

Now that he had his answer, the metro editor didn't seem to know what to do with it. It seemed to be more than he'd bargained for. At first he just sat there. Then he said, "Let me get this straight. Just how long has this paper been running unconfirmed obituaries?"

"About three months," I said. And as I made this admission I felt a smile on my lips, already there before I could fight it back or dissemble it. It was the rictus of panic, the same smile I'd given my mother when she told me my father had died. But of course the metro editor didn't know that.

He leaned forward in his chair and gave his head a little shake, the way a horse will, and said, "Clean out your desk." I don't think he'd meant to fire me; he looked surprised by his own words. But he didn't take them back.

Givens looked from one to the other of us. "Now hold on here," he said. "Let's not blow this all out of proportion. This is a live-and-learn situation. This isn't something a man should lose his job over."

"He wouldn't have," Mrs. Givens said, "if he'd done it right."

Which was a truth beyond argument.

I cleaned out my desk. As I left the building I saw Givens by the newsstand, watching the door. I didn't see his wife.

He walked up to me, raised his hands, and said, "What can I say? I'm at a loss for words."

"Don't worry about it," I told him.

"I sure as heck didn't mean to get you fired. It wasn't even my idea to come in, if you want to know the truth."

"Forget it. It was my own fault." I was carrying a box full of notepads and files, several books. It was heavy. I shifted it under my other arm.

"Look," Givens said, "how about I treat you to lunch. What do you say? It's the least I can do."

I looked up and down the street.

"Dolly's gone on home," he said. "How about it?"

I didn't especially want to eat lunch with Givens, but it seemed to mean a lot to him, and I didn't feel ready to go home yet. What would I do there? Sure, I said, lunch sounded fine. Givens asked me if I knew anyplace reasonable nearby. There was a Chinese joint a few doors down, but it was always full of reporters. I didn't want to watch them try to conjure up sympathy over my situation, which they'd laugh about anyway the minute I left, not that I blamed them. I suggested Tad's Steakhouse over by the cable car turnaround. You could get a six-ounce sirloin, salad, and baked potato for a buck twenty-nine. This was 1974.

"I'm not that short," Givens said. But he didn't argue, and that's where we went.

Givens picked at his food, then pushed the plate away and contemplated mine. When I asked if his steak was okay, he said he didn't have much appetite.

"So," I said, "who do you think called it in?"

His head was bent. He looked up at me from under his eyebrows. "Boy, you've got me there. It's a mystery."

"You must have some idea."

"Nope. Not a one."

"Think it could've been someone you worked with?"

"Nah." He shook a toothpick out of the dispenser. His hands were pale and sinewy.

"It had to be somebody who knows you. You have friends, right?"

"Sure."

"Maybe you had an argument, something like that. Somebody's mad at you."

He kept his mouth covered with one hand while he worked the toothpick with the other. "You think so? I had it figured for more of a joke."

"Well, it's a pretty serious joke, calling in a death notice on someone. Pretty threatening. I'd sure feel threatened, if it was me."

Givens inspected the toothpick, then dropped it in the ashtray. "I hadn't thought of it like that," he said. "Maybe you're right."

I could see he didn't believe it for a second—didn't understand what had happened. The words of death had been pronounced on him, and now his life would be lived in relation to those words, in failing opposition to them, until they overpowered him and became true. Someone had put a contract out on Givens, with words as the torpedoes. Or so it appeared to me.

"You're sure it isn't one of your friends," I said. "It could be a little thing. You played cards, landed some big ones, then folded early before he had a chance to recoup."

"I don't play cards," Givens said.

"How about your wife? Any problems in that department?"

"Nope."

"Everything smooth as silk, huh?"

He shrugged. "Same as ever."

"How come you call her Dolly? That wasn't the name in the obit."

"No reason. I've always called her that. Everybody does."

"I don't feature her as a Dolly," I said.

He didn't answer. He was watching me.

"Let's say Dolly gets mad at you, really mad . . . She wants to send you a message—something outside normal channels."

"Not a chance." Givens said this without bristling. He didn't try to convince me, so I figured he was probably right.

"You're survived by a daughter, right? What's her name again?"

"Tina," he said, with some tenderness.

"That's it, Tina. How are things with Tina?"

"We've had our problems. But I can guarantee you, it wasn't her."

"Well, hell's bells," I said. "Somebody did it."

I finished my steak, watching the show outside: winos, evangelists, outpatients, whores, fake hippies selling oregano to tourists in white shoes. Pure theater, even down to the smell of popcorn billowing out of Woolworth's. Richard Brautigan often came here. Tall and owlish, he stooped to his food and ate slowly, ruminating over every bite, his eyes on the street. Some funny things happened here, and some appalling things. Brautigan took it all in and never stopped eating.

I told Givens that we were sitting at the same table where Richard Brautigan sometimes sat.

"Sorry?"

"Richard Brautigan, the writer."

Givens shook his head.

I was ready to go home. "Okay," I said, "you tell me. Who wants you dead?"

"No one wants me dead."

"Somebody's imagining you dead. Thinking about it. The wish is father to the deed."

"Nobody wants me dead. Your problem is, you think everything has to mean something."

That was one of my problems, I couldn't deny it.

"Just out of curiosity," he said, "what did you think of it?"

"Think of what?"

"My obituary." He leaned forward and started fooling with the salt and pepper shakers, tapping them together and sliding them around like partners in a square dance. "I mean, did you get any feeling for who I was? The kind of person I am?"

I shook my head.

"Nothing stood out?"

I said no.

"I see. Maybe you wouldn't mind telling me, what exactly does it take for you to remember someone?"

"Look," I said, "you write obituaries all day, they sort of blur into each other."

"Yes, but you must remember some of them."

"Some of them—sure."

"Which ones?"

"Writers I like. Great baseball players. Movie stars I've been in love with."

"Celebrities, in other words."

"Some of them, yes. Not all."

"You can lead a good life without being a celebrity," he said. "People with big names aren't always big people."

"That's true," I said, "but it's sort of a little person's truth."

"Is that so? And what does that make you?"

I didn't answer.

"If the only thing that impresses you is having a big name, then you must be a regular midget. At least that's the way I see it." He gave me a hard look and gripped the salt and pepper shakers like a machine gunner about to let off a burst.

"That's not the only thing that impresses me."

"Oh yeah? What else, then?"

I let the question settle. "Moral distinction," I said.

He repeated the words. They sounded pompous.

"You know what I mean," I said.

"Correct me if I'm wrong," he said, "but I have a feeling that's not your department, moral distinction."

I didn't argue.

"And you're obviously not a celebrity."

"Obviously."

"So where does that leave you?" When I didn't answer, he said, "Think you'd remember your own obituary?"

"Probably not."

"No probably about it! You wouldn't even give it a second thought."

"Okay, definitely not."

"You wouldn't even give it a second thought. And you'd be wrong. Because you probably have other qualities that would stand out if you were looking closely. Good qualities. Everybody has something. What do you pride yourself on?"

"I'm a survivor," I said. But I didn't think that claim would carry much weight in an obituary.

Givens said, "With me it's loyalty. Loyalty is a very clear pattern in my life. You would've noticed that if you'd had your eyes open. When you read that a man has served his country in time of war, stayed married to the same woman forty-two years, worked at the same job, by God, that should tell you something. That should give you a certain picture."

He stopped to nod at his own words. "And it hasn't always been easy," he said.

I had to laugh, mostly at myself for being such a dim bulb. "It was you," I said. "You did it."

"Did what?"

"Called in the obit."

"Why would I do that?"

"You tell me."

"That would be saying I did it." Givens couldn't help smiling, proud of what a slyboots he was.

I said, "You're out of your ever-loving mind," but I didn't mean it. There was nothing in what Givens had done that I couldn't make sense of or even, in spite of myself, admire. He had dreamed up a way of going to his own funeral. He'd tried on his last suit, so to speak, seen himself rouged up and laid out, and listened to his own eulogy. And the best part was, he resurrected afterward. That was the real point, even if he thought he was doing it to throw a scare into Dolly or put his virtues on display. Resurrection was what it was all about, and this tax collector had gotten himself a taste of it. It was biblical.

"You're a caution, Mr. Givens. You're a definite caution."

"I didn't come here to be insulted."

"Relax," I told him. "I'm not mad."

He scraped his chair back and stood up. "I've got better things to do than sit here and listen to accusations."

I followed him outside. I wasn't ready to let him go. He had to give me something first. "Admit you did it," I said.

He turned away and started up Powell.

"Just admit it," I said. "I won't hold it against you."

He kept walking, head stuck forward in that turtlish way, navigating the crowd. He was slippery and fast. Finally I took his arm and pulled him into a doorway. His muscles bunched under my fingers. He almost jerked free, but I tightened my grip and we stood there frozen in contention.

"Admit it."

He shook his head.

"I'll break your neck if I have to," I told him.

"Let go," he said.

"If something happened to you right now, your obituary would be solid news. Then I could get my job back."

He tried to pull away again but I held him there.

"It'd make a hell of a story," I said.

I felt his arm go slack. Then he said, almost inaudibly, "Yes." Just that one word.

This was the best I was going to get out of him. It had to be enough. When I let go of his arm he turned and ducked his head and took his place in the stream of people walking past. I started back to Tad's for my box. Just ahead of me a mime was following a young swell in a three-piece suit, catching to the life his leading-man's assurance, the supercilious tilt of his chin. A girl laughed raucously. The swell looked back and the mime froze. He was still holding his pose as I came by. I slipped him a quarter, hoping he'd let me pass.

Casualty

B.D. carried certain objects. He observed in his dispositions and arrangements a certain order, and became irritable and fearful whenever that order was disrupted. There were certain words he said to himself at certain moments, power words. Sometimes he really believed in all of this; other times he believed in nothing. But he was alive, and he gave honor to all possible causes.

His name was Benjamin Delano Sears, B.D. for short, but his friends in the unit had taken to calling him Biddy because of his fussiness and the hennish way he brooded over them. He always had to know where they were. He bugged them about taking their malaria pills and their salt tablets. When they were out in the bush he drove them crazy with equipment checks. He acted like a squad leader, which he wasn't and never would be, because Sergeant Holmes refused to consider him for the job. Sergeant Holmes had a number of sergeant-like sayings. One of them was "If you don't got what it takes, it'll take what you gots." He had decided that B.D. didn't have what it took, and B.D. didn't argue; he knew even better than Sergeant Holmes how scared he was. He just wanted to get himself home, himself and his friends.

Most of them did get home. The unit had light casualties during B.D.'s tour, mainly through dumb luck. One by one B.D.'s friends rotated stateside, and finally Ryan was the only one left. B.D. and Ryan had arrived the same week. They knew the same stories. The names of absent men and past operations and nowhere places had meaning for them, and those who came later began to regard the pair of them as some kind of cultish remnant. And that was pretty much how B.D. and Ryan saw themselves.

They hadn't started off as friends. Ryan was a lip, a big mouth. He narrated whatever was happening, like a sportscaster, but the narration never fit what was going on. He'd complain when operations got canceled, go into fey French-accented ecstasies over cold C-rats, offer elaborate professions of admiration for orders of the most transparent stupidity. At first B.D. thought he was a pain in the ass. Then one morning he woke up laughing at something Ryan had said the night before. They'd been setting out claymores. Sergeant Holmes got exasperated fiddling with one of them and said, "Any you boys gots a screwdriver?" and Ryan said, instantly, "What size?" This was regulation blab, but it worked on B.D. He kept hearing Ryan's voice, its crispness and competence, its almost perfect imitation of sanity.

What size?

Ryan and B.D. had about six weeks left to go when Lieutenant Puchinsky, their commanding officer, got transferred to battalion headquarters. Pinch Puchinsky saw himself as a star—he'd been a quarterback at Penn State, spoiled, coddled, illegally subsidized—and he took it for granted that other men would see him the same way. And they did. He never had to insist on an order and never thought to insist, because he couldn't imagine anyone refusing. He couldn't imagine anything disagreeable, in fact, and carried himself through every danger as if it had nothing to do with him. Because hardly any of his men got hurt, they held him in reverence.

So it was in the nature of things that his replacement, Lieutenant Dixon, should be despised, though he was not despicable. He was a proud, thoughtful man who had been wounded twice already and now found himself among soldiers whose laxity seemed perfectly calculated to finish him off. The men didn't maintain their weapons properly. They had no concept of radio discipline. On patrol they were careless and noisy and slow to react. Lieutenant Dixon took it upon himself to whip them into shape.

This proved hard going. He owned no patience or humor, no ease of command. He was short and balding; when he got worked up his face turned red and his voice broke into falsetto. Therefore the men called him Fudd. Ryan mimicked him relentlessly and with terrible precision. That Lieutenant Dixon should overhear him was inevitable, and it finally happened while Ryan and B.D. and some new guys were sandbagging the interior walls of a bunker. Ryan was holding forth in Lieutenant Dixon's voice when Lieutenant Dixon's head appeared in the doorway. Everyone saw him. But instead of shutting up, Ryan carried on as if he weren't there. B.D. kept his head down and his hands busy. At no time was he tempted to laugh.

"Ryan," lieutenant Dixon said, "just what do you think you're doing?"

Still in the lieutenant's voice, Ryan said, "Packing sandbags, sir."

Lieutenant Dixon watched him. He said, "Ryan, is this your idea of a j-joke?"

"No, sir. My idea of a j-joke is a four-inch dick on a two-inch lieutenant."

B.D. closed his eyes, and when he opened them Lieutenant Dixon was gone. He straightened up. "Suave," he said to Ryan.

Ryan pushed his shovel into the dirt and leaned against it. He untied the bandana from his forehead and wiped the sweat from his face, from his thin shoulders and chest. His ribs showed. His skin was dead white, all but his hands and neck and face, which were densely freckled, almost black in the dimness of the bunker. "I just can't help it," he said.

Three nights later Lieutenant Dixon sent Ryan out on ambush with a bunch of new guys. This was strictly contrary to the arrangement observed by Lieutenant Puchinsky, whereby the shorter you got the less you had to do. You weren't supposed to get stuck with this kind of duty when you had less than two months to go. Lieutenant Dixon did not exactly order Ryan out. What he did instead was turn to him during the noon formation and ask if he'd like to volunteer. Ryan said that he would *love* to volunteer, that he'd been just *dying* to be asked. Lieutenant Dixon put his name down.

B.D. watched the detail go out that night. With blackened faces they moved silently through the perimeter, weaving a loopy path between mines and trip-flares, and crossed the desolate ground beyond the wire into the darkness of the trees. The sky was a lilac haze.

B.D. went back to his bunk and sat there with his hands on his knees, staring at the mess on Ryan's bunk: shaving gear, cigarettes, dirty clothes, sandals, a high-school yearbook that Ryan liked to browse in. B.D. lifted the mosquito netting and picked up the yearbook. *The Aloysian*, it was called. There was a formal portrait of Ryan in the senior class gallery. He looked solemn, almost mournful. His hair was long. The photographer had airbrushed the freckles out and used backlights to brighten the outline of his head and shoulders. B.D. wouldn't have known him without the name. Below Ryan's picture was the line "O for a beakerful of the warm South!"

Now what the hell was that supposed to mean?

He found Ryan in a few group pictures. In one, taken in metal shop, Ryan was standing with some other boys behind the teacher, holding a tangle of antlerish rods above the teacher's head.

B.D. studied the picture. He was familiar with this expression, the plausible blandness worn like a mask over cunning and mockery. It made B.D. want to catch Ryan's eye and let him know that he saw what was going on. He put the book back on Ryan's bed.

His stomach hurt. It was a new pain, not sharp but steady, and so diffuse that B.D. had to probe with his fingers to find its source. When he bent over the pain got worse, then eased up when he stood and walked back and forth in front of his bunk. One of the new guys, a big Hawaiian, said, "Hey, Biddy, you okay?" B.D. stopped pacing. He had forgotten there was anyone else in the room. This Hawaiian and a guy with a green eyeshade and a bunch of others were playing cards. They were all watching him.

B.D. said, "Haven't you read the surgeon-general's warning?"

The Hawaiian looked down at his cigarette.

"Fuckin' Biddy," said the man with the eyeshade, as if B.D. wasn't there. "Eight months I've been in this shithole and he's still calling me *new guy*."

"Ryan calls me Tonto," the Hawaiian said. "Do I look

like an Indian? Seriously, man, do I look like an Indian?"

"You don't exactly look like a white man."

"Yeah? Well I don't *even* look like an Indian, okay?"

"Call him Kemo Sabe. See how he likes that."

"Ryan? He'd love it."

B.D. walked toward Sergeant Holmes's hooch. The sky was low and heavy. They'd had hamburgers that night for dinner, "ratburgers," Ryan called them (*Hey, Cookie, how about tucking in the tail on this one?*), and the air still smelled of grease. B.D. felt a sudden coldness on his back and dropped to a crouch, waiting for something; he didn't know what. He heard the chugging of generators, crumple and thud of distant artillery, the uproarious din of insects. B.D. huddled there. Then he stood and looked around and went on his way.

Sergeant Holmes was stretched out on his bunk, listening to a big reel-to-reel through a set of earphones that covered his head like a helmet. He had on red Bermuda shorts. His eyes were closed, his long spidery fingers waving languorously over his sunken belly. He had the blackest skin B.D. had ever seen on anyone. B.D. sat down beside him and shook his foot. "Hey," he said. "Hey, Russ."

Sergeant Holmes opened his eyes, then slowly pulled the earphones off.

"Dixon has no business sending Ryan out on ambush."

Sergeant Holmes sat up and put the earphones on the floor. "You wrong about that. That's what the man's business is, is sending people out."

"Ryan's been out. Plenty. He's under two months now."

"Same-same you, right?"

B.D. nodded.

"I see why you worried."

"Fuck you," B.D. said.

Sergeant Holmes grinned. It was an event in that black face.

"This goes against the deal, Russ."

"Deal? What's this deal shit? You got something on paper?"

"It was understood."

"Eltee Pinch gone, Biddy. Eltee Dixon head rat-catcher now, and he got his own different philosophy."

"Philosophy," B.D. said.

"That's how it is," Sergeant Holmes said.

B.D. sat there, looking at the floor, rubbing his knuckles. "What do you think?"

"I think Lieutenant Dixon in charge now."

"The new guys can take care of themselves. *We* did."

"You did shit, Biddy. You been duckin' ever since you got here, you and Ryan both."

"We took our chances."

"Hey, that's how it is, Biddy. You don't like it, talk to the Eltee." He pulled his earphones on, lay back on the bunk and closed his eyes. His fingers waved in the air like seaweed.

A few days later Lieutenant Dixon put together another ambush patrol. Before reading off the names he asked if one of the short-timers would like to volunteer. Nobody answered. Everyone was quiet, waiting. Lieutenant Dixon studied his clipboard, wrote something, and looked up. "Right. So who's going?" When no one spoke he said, "Come on, it isn't all that bad. Is it, Ryan?"

B.D. was standing next to him. "Don't answer," he whispered.

"It's just great!" Ryan said. "Nothing like it, sir. You've got your stars twinkling up there in God's heaven—"

"Thanks," Lieutenant Dixon said.

"The trees for company—"

"Shut up," B.D. said.

But Ryan kept at it until Lieutenant Dixon got impatient and cut him off. "That's fine," he said, then added, "I'm glad to hear you like it so much."

"Can't get enough of it, sir."

Lieutenant Dixon slapped the clipboard against his leg. He did it again. "So I guess you wouldn't mind having another crack at it."

"Really, sir? Can I?"

"I think it can be arranged."

B.D. followed Ryan to their quarters after lunch. Ryan was laying out his gear. "I know, I know," he said. "I just can't help it."

"You can keep your mouth shut. You can stop hard-assing the little fuck."

"The thing is, I can't. I try to but I can't."

"Bullshit," B.D. said, but he saw that Ryan meant it, and the knowledge made him tired. He lowered himself onto his bunk and lay back and stared up at the canvas roof. Sunlight spangled in a thousand little holes.

"He's such an asshole," Ryan said. "Somebody's got to brief him on that, because he just doesn't get the picture. He doesn't have *any* hard intelligence on what an asshole he is. Somebody around here's got to take responsibility."

"Nobody assigned you," B.D. said.

"Individual initiative," Ryan said. He sat down on his footlocker and began tinkering with the straps of his helmet.

B.D. closed his eyes. The air was hot and pressing and smelled of the canvas overhead, a smell that reminded him of summer camp.

"But that's not really it," Ryan said. "I'd just as soon let it drop. I think I've made my point."

"Affirmative. Rest assured."

"It's like I'm allergic—you know, like some people are with cats? I get near him and boom! my heart starts pumping like crazy and all this stuff starts coming out. I'm just standing there, watching it happen. Strange, huh? Strange but true."

"All you have to do," B.D. said hopelessly, "is keep quiet."

The power of an M-26 fragmentation grenade, sufficient by itself to lift the roof off a small house, could be "exponentially enhanced," according to a leaflet issued by the base commander, "by detonating it in the context of volatile substances." This absurdly overwritten leaflet, intended as a warning against the enemy practice of slipping delay-rigged grenades into the gas tanks of unattended jeeps and trucks, was incomprehensible to half the men in the division. But B.D. had understood it, and he'd kept it in mind.

His idea was to pick up a five-gallon can of gasoline from one of the generators and leave it beside the tent where Lieutenant Dixon did his paperwork at night. He would tape down the handle of a grenade, pull the pin, and drop the grenade in the can. By the time the gas ate through the tape he'd be in his bunk.

B.D. didn't think he had killed anyone yet. His company had been ambushed three times and B.D. had fired back with everyone else, but always hysterically and in a kind of fog. Something happened to his vision; it turned yellow and blurry and he saw everything in a series of stuttering frames that he could never afterward remember clearly. He couldn't be sure what had happened. But he thought he'd know if he had killed somebody, even if it was in darkness or behind cover where he couldn't see the man go down. He was sure that he would know.

Only once did he remember having someone actually in

his sights. This was during a sweep through an area that had been cleared of its population and declared a free-fire zone. Nobody was supposed to be there. All morning they worked their way upriver, searching empty hamlets along the bank. Nothing. Negative booby traps, negative snipers, negative mines. Zilch. But then, while they were eating lunch, B.D. saw something. He was on guard in the rear of the company when a man came out of the trees into an expanse of overgrown paddies. The man had a stick that he swung in front of him as he made his way with slow, halting steps toward the opposite tree line. B.D. kept still and watched him. The sun was warm on his back. The breeze blew across the paddies, bending the grass, rippling the water. Finally he raised his rifle and drew a bead on the man. He held him in his sights. He could have dropped him, easy as pie, but he decided that the man was blind. He let him go and said nothing about it. But later he wondered: What if he wasn't blind? What if he was just a guy with a stick, taking his time? Either way, he had no business being there. B.D. felt funny about the whole thing. What if he was actually VC, what if he killed a bunch of Americans afterward? He could be VC even if he *was* blind; he could be cadre, infrastructure, some high official . . .

Blind people could do all kinds of things.

Once it got dark B.D. walked across the compound to one of the guard bunkers and palmed a grenade from an open crate while pretending to look for a man named Walcott.

He was about to leave when pumpkin-headed Captain Kroll appeared wheezing in the doorway. He had a normal enough body, maybe a little plump but nothing freakish, and then this incredible head. His head was so big that everyone in camp knew who he was and generally treated him with a tolerance he might not have enjoyed if his head had been a little smaller. "Captain Head," they called him, or just "The Head." He worked in battalion intelligence, which was good for a few laughs, and didn't seem to realize just how big his head really was.

Captain Kroll crouched on the floor and had everyone bunch up around him; it was like a football huddle. B.D. saw no choice but to join in. Captain Kroll looked into each of their faces, and in a hushed voice he said that their reconnaissance patrols were reporting *beaucoup* troop movements all through the valley. They should maintain an extreme degree of alertness, he said. Mister Charles needed some scalps to show off in Paris. Mister Charles was looking for a party.

"Rock and roll!" said the guy behind B.D.

It was a dumbfuck thing to say. Nobody else said a word.

"Any questions?"

No questions.

Captain Kroll rolled his big head from side to side. "Get some," he said.

Everyone broke out laughing.

Captain Kroll rocked back as if he'd been slapped, then stood and left the bunker. B.D. followed him outside and struck off in the opposite direction. The grenade knocked against his hip as he wandered, dull and thoughtless, across the compound. He didn't know where he was going until he got there.

Lieutenant Puchinsky was drinking beer with a couple of other officers. B.D. stood in the doorway of the hooch. "Sir, it's Biddy," he said. "Biddy Sears."

"Biddy?" Lieutenant Puchinsky leaned forward and squinted at him. "Christ. Biddy." He put his can down.

They walked a little ways. Lieutenant Puchinsky gave off a certain ripeness, distinct but not rank, that B.D. had forgotten and now remembered and breathed in, taking comfort from it as he took comfort from the man's bulk, the great looming mass of him.

Lieutenant Puchinsky stopped beside a cyclone fence enclosing a pit filled with crates. "You must be getting pretty short," he said.

"Thirty-four and a wake-up."

"I'm down to twenty."

"Twenty. Jesus, sir. That's all right. I could handle twenty."

A flare burst over the dead space outside the wire. Both men shrank from the sudden brightness. The flare drifted slowly down, hissing as it fell, covering the camp with a cold green light in which everything took on a helpless, cringing aspect. They didn't speak until it came to ground.

"Ours," Lieutenant Puchinsky said.

"Yes, sir," B.D. said, though he knew this might not be true.

Lieutenant Puchinsky shifted from foot to foot.

"It's about Lieutenant Dixon, sir."

"Oh, Christ. You're *not* going to tell me you're having trouble with Lieutenant Dixon."

"Yes, sir."

When Lieutenant Puchinsky asked if he'd gone through channels, B.D. knew he'd already lost his case. He tried to explain the situation but couldn't find the right words, and Lieutenant Puchinsky kept interrupting to say that it wasn't his outfit anymore. He wouldn't even admit that an injustice had been done since Ryan had, after all, volunteered.

"Lieutenant Dixon made him," B.D. said.

"How was that?"

"I can't explain, sir. He has a way."

Lieutenant Puchinsky didn't say anything.

"We did what you wanted," B.D. said. "We kept our part of the deal."

"There weren't any deals," Lieutenant Puchinsky said. "It sounds to me like you've got a personal problem, soldier. If your mission requires personal problems, we'll issue them to you. Is that clear?"

"Yes, sir."

"If you're so worried about him, why don't *you* volunteer?"

B.D. came to attention, snapped a furiously correct salute, and turned away.

"Hold up, Biddy." Lieutenant Puchinsky walked over to him. "What do you expect me to do? Put yourself in my place—what am I supposed to do?"

"You could talk to him."

"It won't do any good, I can guarantee you that." When B.D. didn't answer, he said, "All right. If it makes you feel any better, I'll talk to him."

B.D. did feel better, but not for long.

He had trouble sleeping that night, and as he lay in the darkness, eyes open, a rusty taste in his mouth, the extent of his failure became clear to him. He knew exactly what would happen. Lieutenant Puchinsky thought he was going to talk to Lieutenant Dixon, and he would be loyal to this intention for maybe an hour or two, maybe even the rest of the night, and in the morning he'd forget it. He was an officer. Officers could look like men and talk like men, but when you drew the line they always went over to the officer side because that was what they were. Lieutenant Puchinsky had already decided that speaking to Lieutenant Dixon wouldn't make any difference. And he was right. B.D. knew that. He understood that he had known it all along, that he'd gone to Lieutenant Puchinsky so he wouldn't be able to deal with Lieutenant Dixon afterward. He'd tipped his hand because he was afraid to play it, and now the chance was gone. In another four or five days, the next time battalion sent down for an ambush party, Lieutenant Dixon would be out there asking for a volunteer, and Ryan would shoot off his mouth again.

And Lieutenant Puchinsky thought that he, B.D., should go out instead.

B.D. lay on his back for a while, then turned on his side. It was hot. Finally he got up and went to the doorway of the hooch. A new guy was sitting there in his boxer shorts, smoking a pipe. He nodded at B.D. but didn't say anything. There was no breeze. B.D. stood in the doorway, then went back inside and sat on his bunk.

B.D. wasn't brave. He knew that, as he knew other things about himself that he would not have believed a year ago. He would not have believed that he could walk past begging children and feel nothing. He would not have believed that he could become a frequenter of prostitutes. He would not have believed that he could become a whiner or a shirker. He had been forced to surrender certain pictures of himself that had once given him pride and a serene sense of entitlement to his existence, but the one picture he had not given up, and which had become essential to him, was the picture of himself as a man who would do anything for a friend.

Anything meant anything. It could mean getting himself hurt or even killed. B.D. had some ideas as to how this might happen, acts of impulse like going after a wounded man, jumping on a grenade, other things he'd heard and read about, and in which he thought he recognized the possibilities of his own nature. But this was different.

In fact, B.D. could see a big difference. It was one thing to do something in the heat of the moment, another to think about it, accept it in advance. Anything meant anything, but B.D. never thought it would mean volunteering for an ambush party. He'd pulled that duty and hated it worse than anything. You had to lie out there all night without moving. When you thought a couple of hours had gone by, it turned out to be fifteen minutes. You couldn't see a thing. You had to figure it all out with your ears, and every sound made you want to blow the whole place apart, but you couldn't because then they'd know where you were. Then they had you. Or else some friendly unit heard the firing and got spooked and called down artillery. That happened once when B.D. was out; some guys freaked and shot the shit out of some bushes, and it wasn't three minutes before the artillery started coming in. B.D. had been mortared but he'd never been under artillery before. Artillery was something else. Artillery was like the end of the world. It was a miracle he hadn't gotten killed—a miracle. He didn't know if he was up for that again. He just didn't know.

B.D. rummaged in Ryan's stuff for some cigarettes. He lit one and puffed it without inhaling, blowing the smoke over his head; he hated the smell of it. The men around him slept on, their bodies pale and vague under the mosquito-netting. B.D. ground the cigarette out and lay down again.

He didn't know Ryan all that well, when you came right down to it. The things he knew about Ryan he could count on his fingers. Ryan was nineteen. He had four older sisters, no brothers, a girlfriend he never talked about. What he did like to talk about was driving up to New Hampshire with his buddies and fishing for trout. He was clumsy. He talked too much. He could eat anything, even gook food. He called the black guys Zulus but got along with them better than B.D., who claimed to be color-blind. His mother was dead. His father ran a hardware store and picked up the odd dollar singing nostalgic Irish songs at weddings and wakes. Ryan could do an imitation of his father singing that put B.D. right on the floor, every time. It was something he did with his eyebrows. Just thinking of it made B.D. laugh silently in the darkness.

Ryan was on a supply detail that weekend, completely routine, carrying ammunition forward from a dump in the rear, when a machine gun opened fire from a low hill that was supposed to be secure. It caught Ryan and several other men as they were humping crates across a mudfield. The whole area went on alert. Perimeter guards were blasting away at the hill. Officers kept running by, shouting different orders.

When B.D. heard about Ryan he left his position and took off running toward the LZ. There were two wounded men there, walking wounded, and a corpse in a bag, but Ryan was gone. He'd been lifted out with the other criticals a few minutes earlier. The medic on duty said that Ryan had taken a round just above the left eye, or maybe it was the right. He didn't know how serious it was, whether the bullet had hit him straight on or from the side.

B.D. looked up at the sky, at the dark, low, eddying clouds. He was conscious of the other men, and he clenched his jaw to show that he was keeping a tight lid on his feelings, as he was. Years later he told all this to the woman he lived with and would later marry, offering it to her as something important to know about him—how this great friend of his, Ryan, had gotten hit, and how he'd run to be with him and found him gone. He described the scene in the clearing, the wounded men sitting on tree stumps, muddy, dumb with shock, and the dead man in his bag, not stretched out like someone asleep but all balled up in the middle. A big lump. He described the churned-up ground, the jumble of boxes and canisters. The dark sky. And Ryan gone, just like that. His best friend.

This story did not come easily to B.D. He hardly ever talked about the war except in generalities, and then in a grudging, edgy way. He didn't want to sound like other men when they got on the subject, pulling a long face or laughing it off—striking a pose. He did not want to imply that he'd done more than he had done, or to say, as he believed, that he hadn't done enough; that all he had done was stay alive. When he thought about those days, the life he'd led since—working his way through school, starting a business, being a good friend to his friends, nursing his mother for three months while she died of cancer—all this dropped away as if it were nothing, and he felt as he had felt then, weak, corrupt, and afraid.

So B.D. avoided the subject.

Still, he knew that his silence had become its own kind of pose, and that was why he told his girlfriend about Ryan. He wanted to be truthful with her. What a surprise, then, to have it all come out sounding like a lie. He couldn't get it right, couldn't put across what he had felt. He used the wrong words, words that somehow rang false, in sentimental cadences. The details sounded artful. His voice was halting and grave, self-aware, phony. It embarrassed him and he could see that it was embarrassing her, so he stopped. B.D. concluded that grief was impossible to describe.

But that was not why he failed. He failed because he had not felt grief that day, finding Ryan gone. He had felt delivered—set free. He couldn't recognize it, let alone admit it, but that's what it was, a strong, almost disabling sense of release. It took him by surprise but he fought it down, mastered it before he knew what it was, thinking it must be something else. He took charge of himself as necessity decreed. When the next chopper came in, B.D. helped the medic put the corpse and the wounded men on board, and then he went back to his position. It was starting to rain.

A doctor in Qui Nhon did what he could for Ryan and then tagged him for shipment to Japan. That night they loaded him onto a C-141 med evac bound for Yokota, from there to be taken to the hospital at Zama. The ride was rough at first because of driving winds and the steep, almost corkscrew turns the pilot had to make to avoid groundfire from around the airfield. The nurses crouched in the aisle, gripping the frames of the berths as the plane pitched and yawed. The lights flickered. IV bags swung from their hooks. Men cried out. In this way they spiraled upward until they gained the thin, cold, untroubled heights, and then the pilot set his course, and the men mostly quieted down, and the nurses went about their business.

One heard Ryan say something as she passed his cot. She knelt beside him and he said it again, a word she couldn't make out. She took his pulse, monitored his breathing: shallow but regular. The dressing across his forehead and face was soaked through. She changed it, but had to leave the seeping compress on the wound; the orders on the chart specified that no one should touch it until he reached a certain team of doctors in Zama. When she'd finished with the dressing the nurse began to wipe his face. "Come on in," Ryan said, and seized her hand.

It gave her a start. "What?" she said.

He didn't speak again. She let him hold her hand until his grasp loosened, but when she tried to pull away he clamped down again. His lips moved soundlessly.

In the berth next to Ryan's was a boy who'd had both feet blown off. He was asleep, or unconscious; she could see the rise and fall of his chest. His near hand was resting on the deck. She picked it up by the wrist, and when Ryan relaxed his grip again she gave him his neighbor's hand and withdrew her own. He didn't seem to know the difference. She wiped his face once more and went to help another nurse with a patient who kept trying to get up.

She wasn't sure exactly when Ryan died. He was alive at one moment, and when she stopped by again, not so long afterward, he was gone. He still had the other boy's hand. She stood there and looked at them. She couldn't think what to do. Finally she went over to another nurse and took her aside. "I'm going to need a little something after all," she said.

The other nurse looked around. "I don't have any."

"Beth," she said. "Please."

"Don't ask, okay? You made me promise."

"Look," she said, "just this trip. It's all right—really, Beth, I mean it. It's all right."

During a lull later on she stopped and leaned her forehead against a porthole. The sun was just above the horizon. The sky was clear, no clouds between her and the sea below, whose name she loved to hear the pilots say—the East China Sea. Through the crazed Plexiglas she could make out some small islands and the white glint of a ship in the apex of its wake. Someday she was going to take passage on one of those ships, by herself or maybe with some friends. Lie in the sun. Breathe the good air. Do nothing all day but eat and sleep and be clean, throw crumbs to the gulls and watch the dolphins play alongside, diving and then leaping high to show off for the people at the rail, for her and her friends. She could see the whole thing. When she closed her eyes she could see the whole thing, perfectly.

Powder

*J*ust before Christmas my father took me skiing at Mount
Baker. He'd had to fight for the privilege of my company, because my mother was still angry with him for
sneaking me into a nightclub during his last visit, to see
Thelonious Monk.

He wouldn't give up. He promised, hand on heart, to
take good care of me and have me home for dinner on
Christmas Eve, and she relented. But as we were checking
out of the lodge that morning it began to snow, and in this
snow he observed some rare quality that made it necessary
for us to get in one last run. We got in several last runs. He
was indifferent to my fretting. Snow whirled around us in
bitter, blinding squalls, hissing like sand, and still we skied.
As the lift bore us to the peak yet again, my father looked
at his watch and said, "Criminy. This'll have to be a fast
one."

By now I couldn't see the trail. There was no point in
trying. I stuck to him like white on rice and did what he did
and somehow made it to the bottom without sailing off a
cliff. We returned our skis and my father put chains on the
Austin-Healey while I swayed from foot to foot, clapping

my mittens and wishing I was home. I could see everything. The green tablecloth, the plates with the holly pattern, the red candles waiting to be lit.

We passed a diner on our way out. "You want some soup?" my father asked. I shook my head. "Buck up," he said. "I'll get you there. Right, doctor?"

I was supposed to say, "Right, doctor," but I didn't say anything.

A state trooper waved us down outside the resort. A pair of sawhorses were blocking the road. The trooper came up to our car and bent down to my father's window. His face was bleached by the cold. Snowflakes clung to his eyebrows and to the fur trim of his jacket and cap.

"Don't tell me," my father said.

The trooper told him. The road was closed. It might get cleared, it might not. Storm took everyone by surprise. So much, so fast. Hard to get people moving. Christmas Eve. What can you do.

My father said, "Look. We're talking about five, six inches. I've taken this car through worse than that."

The trooper straightened up. His face was out of sight but I could hear him. "The road is closed."

My father sat with both hands on the wheel, rubbing the wood with his thumbs. He looked at the barricade for a long time. He seemed to be trying to master the idea of it. Then he thanked the trooper, and with a weird, old-maidy show of caution turned the car around. "Your mother will never forgive me for this," he said.

"We should have left before," I said. "Doctor."

He didn't speak to me again until we were in a booth at the diner, waiting for our burgers. "She won't forgive me," he said. "Do you understand? Never."

"I guess," I said, but no guesswork was required; she wouldn't forgive him.

"I can't let that happen." He bent toward me. "I'll tell

you what I want. I want us all to be together again. Is that what you want?"

"Yes, sir."

He bumped my chin with his knuckles. "That's all I needed to hear."

When we finished eating he went to the pay phone in the back of the diner, then joined me in the booth again. I figured he'd called my mother, but he didn't give a report. He sipped at his coffee and stared out the window at the empty road. "Come on, come on," he said, though not to me. A little while later he said it again. When the trooper's car went past, lights flashing, he got up and dropped some money on the check. "Okay. Vamanos."

The wind had died. The snow was falling straight down, less of it now and lighter. We drove away from the resort, right up to the barricade. "Move it," my father told me. When I looked at him he said, "What are you waiting for?" I got out and dragged one of the sawhorses aside, then put it back after he drove through. He pushed the door open for me. "Now you're an accomplice," he said. "We go down together." He put the car into gear and gave me a look. "Joke, son."

Down the first long stretch I watched the road behind us, to see if the trooper was on our tail. The barricade vanished. Then there was nothing but snow: snow on the road, snow kicking up from the chains, snow on the trees, snow in the sky; and our trail in the snow. Then I faced forward and had a shock. The lay of the road behind us had been marked by our own tracks, but there were no tracks ahead of us. My father was breaking virgin snow between a line of tall trees. He was humming "Stars Fell on Alabama." I felt snow brush along the floorboards under my feet. To keep my hands from shaking I clamped them between my knees.

My father grunted in a thoughtful way and said, "Don't ever try this yourself."

"I won't."

"That's what you say now, but someday you'll get your license and then you'll think you can do anything. Only you won't be able to do this. You need, I don't know—a certain instinct."

"Maybe I have it."

"You don't. You have your strong points, but not this. I only mention it because I don't want you to get the idea this is something just anybody can do. I'm a great driver. That's not a virtue, okay? It's just a fact, and one you should be aware of. Of course you have to give the old heap some credit, too. There aren't many cars I'd try this with. Listen!"

I did listen. I heard the slap of the chains, the stiff, jerky rasp of the wipers, the purr of the engine. It really did purr. The old heap was almost new. My father couldn't afford it, and kept promising to sell it, but here it was.

I said, "Where do you think that policeman went to?"

"Are you warm enough?" He reached over and cranked up the blower. Then he turned off the wipers. We didn't need them. The clouds had brightened. A few sparse, feathery flakes drifted into our slipstream and were swept away. We left the trees and entered a broad field of snow that ran level for a while and then tilted sharply downward. Orange stakes had been planted at intervals in two parallel lines and my father steered a course between them, though they were far enough apart to leave considerable doubt in my mind as to exactly where the road lay. He was humming again, doing little scat riffs around the melody.

"Okay then. What are my strong points?"

"Don't get me started," he said. "It'd take all day."

"Oh, right. Name one."

"Easy. You always think ahead."

True. I always thought ahead. I was a boy who kept his clothes on numbered hangers to insure proper rotation. I bothered my teachers for homework assignments far ahead of their due dates so I could draw up schedules. I thought ahead, and that was why I knew that there would be other troopers waiting for us at the end of our ride, if we even got there. What I did not know was that my father would wheedle and plead his way past them—he didn't sing "O Tannenbaum," but just about—and get me home for dinner, buying a little more time before my mother decided to make the split final. I knew we'd get caught; I was resigned to it. And maybe for this reason I stopped moping and began to enjoy myself.

Why not? This was one for the books. Like being in a speedboat, only better. You can't go downhill in a boat. And it was all ours. And it kept coming, the laden trees, the unbroken surface of snow, the sudden white vistas. Here and there I saw hints of the road, ditches, fences, stakes, but not so many that I could have found my way. But then I didn't have to. My father was driving. My father in his forty-eighth year, rumpled, kind, bankrupt of honor, flushed with certainty. He was a great driver. All persuasion, no coercion. Such subtlety at the wheel, such tactful pedalwork. I actually trusted him. And the best was yet to come—switchbacks and hairpins impossible to describe. Except maybe to say this: if you haven't driven fresh powder, you haven't driven.

The Life of the Body

Wiley got lonely one night and drove to a bar in North Beach owned by a guy he used to teach with. He watched a basketball game and afterward fell into conversation with the woman sitting next to him. She was a veterinarian. Her name was Kathleen. When Wiley said her name he laid on a bit of the Irish and she smiled at him. She had freckles and very green eyes, "green as the fields of Erin," he told her, and she laughed, holding her head back and deciding—he could tell, he could see it happen—to let things take their course. She was a little drunk. She touched him as she talked, his wrist, his hand, once even his thigh, to drive a point home. Wiley agreed, but he didn't hear what she was saying. There was a rushing sound in his ears.

The man Kathleen had come in with, a short, red-faced, bearded man in a safari jacket, held his glass with both hands and pondered it. He sometimes looked over at Kathleen, at her back. Then he looked at his glass again. Wiley wanted to keep everything friendly, so he leaned forward and stared at him until their eyes met, and then he lifted his glass in salute. The man gaped like a fish. He jabbed his finger at Wiley and yelled something unintelligible. Kathleen turned and took his arm. Then the bartender joined them. He was wiping his hands with a towel. He leaned over the bar and spoke to Kathleen and the short man in a soft voice while Wiley looked on encouragingly.

"That's the ticket," Wiley said. "Talk him down."

The short man jerked his arm away from Kathleen. Kathleen looked around at Wiley and said, "You keep your mouth shut."

The bartender nodded. "Please be quiet," he said.

"Now just a minute," Wiley said.

The bartender ignored him. He went on talking in that soft voice of his. Wiley couldn't follow everything he said, but he did hear words to the effect that he, Wiley, had been drinking hard all night and that they shouldn't take him too seriously.

"Whoa!" Wiley said. "Just hold on a second. I'm having a quiet conversation with my neighbor here, and all of a sudden Napoleon declares war. Why is that my fault?"

"Sir, I asked you to be quiet."

"You ought to cut him off," the short man said.

"I was about to."

"I don't believe this," Wiley said. "For your information, I happen to be a very old friend of Bob's."

"Mr. Lundgren isn't here tonight."

"I can see that. I have eyes. My point is, if Bob were here . . ." Wiley stopped. The three of them were looking at him as if he was a complete asshole, the little guy so superior he wasn't even mad anymore. Wiley had to admit, he sounded like one—dropping the name of a publican, for Christ's sake. A former algebra teacher. "I have many friends in high places," he said, trying to make a joke of it, but they just kept looking at him. They actually thought he was serious. "Oh, relax," he said.

"I'm sure Mr. Lundgren will be happy to take care of

your tab," the bartender said. "If you want to make a complaint he'll be in tomorrow afternoon."

"You can't be serious. Are you throwing me out?"

The bartender considered the question. Then he said, "Right now we're at the request stage."

"But this is ridiculous."

"You're free to leave under your own steam, sir, and I'd be much obliged if you did."

"This is absolutely incredible," Wiley said, more to himself than the bartender, in whose studied courtesy he did not fail to hear the possibility of competent violence. But he was damned if he was going to be hurried. He finished his drink and set the glass down. He slid off his stool, inclined his head toward Kathleen, gravely thanked her for the pleasure of her company. He crossed the room with perfect dignity and stepped outside, taking care that the door should not slam behind him.

A cold light rain was falling. Wiley stood under the awning and hopelessly waited for it to stop. From the place across the street he heard a woman laugh loudly; he thought of lipstick-stained teeth, a pink tongue licking off the creamy mustache left by a White Russian. He leaned in that direction, thrusting his head forward as he did when he caught certain smells in the breeze—curry, roasting coffee, baking bread. Wiley raised his jacket collar and pushed off up the hill, toward the garage where he'd left his car. When he reached the corner he stopped. He couldn't go home now, not like this. He could not allow this absurd picture of himself to survive in Kathleen's mind. It was important that she know the truth about him, and not go through life believing that he was some kind of mouthy lush who got tossed out of bars. Because he wasn't. This had never happened to him before.

He crossed the street and walked back downhill to the other bar. Two women were sitting in the corner with three men. The one Wiley had heard laughing was still at it. Whenever anybody said anything she cracked up. They were all in their fifties, tourists by the look of them, the only customers in the place. Wiley bought a whisky and carried it to a table by the window where he could keep an eye on the bar he'd just been asked to leave.

Nothing like this had ever happened to him. He was an English teacher in a private high school. He lived alone. He didn't go to bars much and almost never drank whisky. He liked good wine, knew something about it, but was wary of knowing too much. At night, after he'd prepared his classes, he drank wine and read nineteenth-century novels. He didn't like modern fiction, its narcissism, its moral timidity, its silence in the face of great wrongs. Wiley had started teaching to support himself while he wrote his doctoral thesis, and then lost interest in scholarship as he began to sense the power of his position. His students were still young enough not to be captive to the lies the world told about itself; he could make a difference in the way they saw things.

Wiley read thick books late into the night and often got only a few hours' sleep, but in nine years he had never missed a day of work; come morning he pushed himself out of bed just in time and drove to school still fumbling with his buttons, stomach empty, coffee sloshing in the cup between his knees.

Wiley didn't like living alone. He wanted to get married, and had always assumed he would be married by now, but he'd had bad luck with women. The last one brushed him off after four months. Her name was Monique. She was a French teacher on exchange, a tall jaunty Parisian who humiliated the boys in her class by mimicking their oafish accents, and the girls by rendering them invisible to the boys. She wore dark glasses even when she went to movies. Her full red lips were habitually pursed. Wiley learned they were held thus in readiness not for passion but scorn, at least where he was concerned. After Monique read *Catcher in the Rye* her dissatisfaction found a home in the word phony. He never understood why she'd settled on him in the first place. Sometimes he thought it was for his language; he liked to talk, and talked well, and Monique was in the states to polish her English. But her reasons were a mystery. She dropped him cold without ever making them clear.

Wiley had finished two whiskies and just bought a third when Kathleen and the little guy came out of the bar. They stopped in the doorway and watched the rain, which was falling harder now. They stood well apart, not speaking, and watched the rain drip off the awning. She looked into her purse, said something to him. He patted his jacket pockets. She rummaged in her purse again and then the two of them ducked their heads and started up the hill. Wiley stood suddenly, knocking his chair over. He picked it up and left the bar.

He had to walk fast. It was an effort. His feet kept taking him from side to side. He bent forward, compelling them to follow. He reached the corner and shouted, "Kathleen!"

She was on the opposite corner. The man was a few steps ahead of her, leaning into the rain. They both stopped and looked over at Wiley. Wiley walked into the street and came toward them. He said, "I love you, Kathleen." He was surprised to hear himself say this, and then to say, as he stepped up on the curb, "Come home with me." She didn't look the way he remembered her. In fact he barely recognized her. She put her hand to her mouth. Wiley couldn't tell whether she was shocked or afraid or what. Maybe she was laughing. He smiled foolishly, confused by his own presence here and by what he'd said, not sure what to say next. Then the little guy came past her and Wiley felt a blow on his cheek and his head snapped back, and right after that the wind went out of him in a whoosh and he folded up, clutching his stomach, unable to breathe or speak. There was another blow at the back of his knees and he fell forward against the curb. He saw a shoe coming at his face and tried to jerk his head away but it caught him just above the eye. He heard Kathleen screaming and the shoe hit him on the mouth. He rolled away and covered his face with his hands. Kathleen kept screaming, *No Mike No Mike No Mike No!* Wiley could feel himself being kicked on his shoulders and back. A dull, faraway pain that went on for a while, and then ceased.

He lay where he was, not trusting the silence, afraid that by moving he would make it all start again. Finally he raised himself to his hands and knees. There was broken glass in the street, glittering on the wet asphalt, and to see it at just this angle, so close, so familiar, so perfectly a part of everything that had happened to him, was to feel utterly reduced; and he knew that he would never forget this, being on his knees with broken glass all around. The rain fell softly. He heard himself weeping, and stopped; it was a stagey, dishonest sound. His lower lip throbbed. He licked it. It was swollen, and tasted of salt and leather.

Wiley stood up, steadying himself against the wall of a building. Two men came toward him, talking excitedly. He was afraid that they would stop to help him, ask him questions. What if they called the police? He had no excuse for his condition, no explanation. Wiley turned his face. The men walked past him as if he wasn't there, or as if he belonged there, in exactly that pose, as part of what they expected a street to look like.

Home. He had to get home. Wiley pushed away from the wall and started walking. He was surprised at how well he walked. His head was clear, his feet steady. He felt exuberant, even exultant, as if he'd gotten away with something. Light and easy. The feeling lasted through most of the drive home, and then it broke; by the time Wiley reached his apartment he was weak and cold, seized by feverish trembling.

He went straight to the bathroom and turned on the light. His lower lip was cut and bleeding, purplish in color, puffed up like a sausage. He had another cut over his left eyebrow, the skin above it scraped raw all the way to his hairline. His chin was bloody and flecked with dirt. He could see a bruise beginning on his cheekbone. My God, he thought, looking at himself. He felt great tenderness for the person behind this lurid mask, as if it were not his face at all, but the face of a beaten child. He touched the hurt places. The raw skin clung to his fingertips.

Wiley took a long bath and tried to sleep, but whenever he closed his eyes he felt a malign presence in the room. In spite of the bath he still felt cold. He got up and looked at himself in the mirror again, hoping to find some change for the better. He inspected his face, then brewed a pot of coffee and spent the rest of the night at the kitchen table, staring blindly at a book and finally sleeping, slumped sideways in the chair, chin on his chest.

When the alarm went off Wiley roused himself and got ready for school. He couldn't think of any reason not to go except embarrassment; and since other teachers would have to cover his classes during their free time, this did not seem a very good reason. But he gave no thought to the effect of his appearance. When the first students saw him in the hallway and started quizzing him, he had no answers ready. One boy asked if he'd been mugged.

Wiley nodded, thinking that was basically true.

"Must have been a whole shitload of them."

"Well, not that many," Wiley said, and walked on. He went straight to his classroom instead of stopping off in the teachers' lounge, but he hadn't been at his desk five minutes before the principal came in.

"Mr. Wiley," he said, "let's have a look at you." He walked up close and peered at Wiley's face. Students were filing in behind him, trying not to stare at Wiley as they took their seats. "What exactly happened?" the principal asked.

"I got mugged."

"Have you seen a doctor?"

"Not yet."

"You should. That's a prize set of bruises you've got there. Very nasty. Call the police?"

"No. I'm still in sort of a daze." Wiley said this in a low voice so the students wouldn't hear him.

Wiley's friend Mac stuck his head in the doorway, nodding coolly at the principal. "You okay?" he said to Wiley.

"I guess."

"I heard there were eight of them. Is that right, eight?"

"No." Wiley tried to smile but his face wouldn't let him. "Just two," he said. He couldn't admit to one, not with all this damage.

"Two's enough," Mac said.

The principal said, "Just let me know if you want to go home. Seriously, now, Mr. Wiley—no heroics. I'm touched that you came in at all." He stopped at the door on his way out and turned to the students. "Be warned, ladies and gentlemen. What happened to Mr. Wiley is going to happen to your children. It will be a common occurrence. That's the kind of world they're going to live in if you don't do something to change it." He let his eyes pass slowly around the room the way he did at school assemblies. "The choice is yours," he said.

Mac applauded silently behind him.

After Mac and the principal left, two boys got up and pretended to attack each other with kicks and chops, crying *Hai! Hai! Hai!* One of them drove the other to the back of the classroom, where he crashed to the floor and sprawled with his arms and legs twitching. Then the bell rang and they both went back to their desks.

This was a senior honors class. The students had been reading "Benito Cereno," one of Wiley's favorite stories, but he had trouble getting a discussion started because of the way they were looking at him. Finally he decided to give a straight lecture. He talked about Melville's exposure of the contradictions in human law, which claims to serve justice while it strengthens the hand of the property owner, even when that property is human. This was one of Wiley's pet subjects, the commodification of humanity. As he warmed to it he forgot the condition of his face and assumed his habitual patrol in front of the class, head bent, hands in his pockets, one eye cocked in a squint. He related this story to the last one they'd read, "Bartleby the Scrivener," quoting with derisory, operatic exaggeration the well-intentioned narrator who cannot understand the truculence of a human being whom he has tried to turn into a Xerox machine. And this was not the voice of some reactionary fascist beast, Wiley said, jingling his keys and change as he paced the room. This was the voice of modern man—modern, enlightened, liberal man.

He had worked himself into that pitch of indignation where everything seemed clear to him, evil and good and all the sly imitations of good that lay in wait for the unwary pilgrim. At such moments he forgot himself entirely. He became Scott Fitzgerald denouncing the foul dust that floated in Gatsby's wake, Jonathan Swift ridiculing bourgeois complacency by suggesting a crime so obscene it took your breath away, yet less obscene than the crimes ordinary people tolerated without a second thought.

And what happened to Bartleby, Wiley said, was only a hint of things to come. "Look at the multinationals!" he said. And then, not for the first time, he described the evolution of business-school theory to its logical conclusion, high-tech factories in the middle of foreign jungles where, behind razor-wire fences guarded by soldiers and dogs, tribesmen who had never seen a flush toilet were made to assemble fax machines and laptop computers. A million Bartlebys, a billion Bartlebys!

Wiley didn't have the documentation on these jungle factories; it was something someone had told him, but it made sense and was right in tune with the spirit of late-twentieth-century capitalism. It sounded true enough to make him furious whenever he talked about it. He finished his lecture with only a few minutes to go before the bell. He felt very professional. It was no mean feat, getting your ass kicked at two in the morning and giving a dynamite lecture at nine. He asked his students if they had any questions. None of them did, at first. Wiley heard whispers. Then a girl raised her hand, shyly, almost as if she hoped he wouldn't notice. When Wiley called on her she looked at the boy across the aisle, Robbins, and said, "What color were they?"

Wiley did not understand the question. She looked over at Robbins again. Robbins said, "They were black, right?"

"Who?"

"The guys that jumped you."

Wiley had always liked this boy and expected him to learn something in here, to think better thoughts than his FBI-agent father who griped to the principal about Wiley's reading list. Wiley leaned against the blackboard. "I don't know," he said.

"Yeah, right," Robbins said.

"I really don't think so," Wiley said. This sounded improbably vague even to him, so he added, "It was dark. I couldn't see them."

Robbins gave a great shout of laughter. Some of the other students laughed too; then one of them hit a wild note that sent everyone into a kind of fit. "Quiet!" Wiley said, but they kept laughing. They were beyond his reach; all he could do was stand there and wait for them to stop. Wiley had three black students in this class, two girls and a boy. They stared at their books in exactly the same way, as if by agreement, though they were sitting in different parts of the room. At the beginning of the year they'd always sat together, but now they drifted from desk to desk like everyone else. They seemed to feel at home in his class. And that was what he wanted, for this room to be a sanctuary, a place the rest of the world should be like. There was no other reason for him to be here.

The bell rang. Wiley sat down and rustled through some papers as the students, suddenly and strangely quiet, walked past his desk. Then he went to the office and told the principal he was going home after all. He was feeling terrible, he said.

He slept for a few hours. After he got up he looked through the veterinarians' listings in the yellow pages and found a Dr. Kathleen Newman on the staff of a clinic specializing in surgery on exotic pets. He called the clinic and asked for Dr. Newman. The man who answered said she was in a meeting. "Is it an emergency?"

"I'm afraid so," Wiley said. "It is sort of an emergency. Tell her," he said, "that Mr. Melville's cetacean has distemper."

Wiley spelled out cetacean for him.

And then a woman's voice was on the line. "Who is this, please?" It was her. But sharp, no fooling around. Wiley couldn't answer. He'd expected her to pick up his joke, and now he didn't know how to begin. "Hello? He*llo*? Damn," she said, and hung up.

Wiley turned to the white pages. There was a Dr. K. P. Newman on Filbert Street. He wrote down the number and address.

Mac's wife, Alice, stopped by that afternoon with bread and salad. She had been a student of Wiley's, and one of his favorites, a pale, slow-moving, thoughtful girl he would never have suspected of carrying on with a teacher, which showed how much he knew; she and Mac had been going strong ever since her junior year. They got married right after she graduated. There was a scandal, of course, and Mac almost lost his job, but somehow it never came to that. Wiley found the whole thing very confusing. He disapproved and was jealous; he felt as if Mac had somehow made a fool of him. But eight years had passed since then.

Alice stopped inside the door and looked at Wiley's face. He saw that she was shocked to the point of tears.

"It'll mend," he told her.

"But why would anyone do that to you?"

"These things happen," he said.

"Well, they shouldn't."

She sent him back to the living room. Wiley lay on the couch and watched her through the kitchen doorway while she set the table and made lunch. He was happy having her to himself in his apartment; it was a wish of his. Alice didn't know he felt that way. When they all went out to bars she sat beside him and leaned her head on his shoulder. She took sips from his drinks. She liked to dance, and when she danced with Wiley she moved right up close, talking all the while about everyday things that somehow made their closeness respectable. At the end of a night out, when Mac and Alice drove Wiley home and came inside to call their sitter and drink a glass of wine, and then another, and Wiley began to read to them some high-minded passage from whatever novel he was caught up in, she would stretch out on the couch and rest her head in Wiley's lap while Mac looked on benignly from the easy chair. Wiley knew that he was supposed to feel honored by all this faith, but he resented it. Faith had become an imposition. It made light of his capacity for desire. Still, he put up with it because he didn't know what else to do.

Now Alice was slicing tomatoes at his kitchen counter. She had a flat-footed way of standing. Her hair was gathered in a bun, but loose strands hung in her face; she blew them away as she worked. She had gained weight over the years, but Wiley liked the little tuck of flesh under her chin, and the plumpness of her hands.

She called him to the table. She was quiet, and when she looked at him she quickly looked down again. Wiley didn't think it was because of his banged-up face, but because they had never been alone before. In all her playfulness with him there was an element of performance, and now she didn't have Mac here to give it irony and keep it safe.

Finally she said, "Do you want some wine with this?"

"No. Thanks."

"Sure?"

He nodded.

She pointed her fork at the empty bottles lined against the wall. "Did you drink all those?"

"Over a period of time."

"Oh, great. I'm glad you didn't drink them all at once. Like what period of time are we talking about?"

"I don't know. I don't keep track of every drink."

"That's the trouble with living alone," she said, as if she knew.

"I guess."

"So how come you didn't marry Monique, anyway?" She gave him a quick sidelong look.

"Monique? Come on. She would've laughed me out of town if I'd even mentioned the subject."

"I thought she was nuts about you."

He shook his head.

"Well, I sure thought she was."

"She wasn't."

"Okay then, what about Lynn?"

"That was crazy, that whole thing with Lynn. I don't even want to talk about Lynn."

"She was pretty spoiled."

"It wasn't her fault. It just got crazy."

"I didn't like her. She was so sarcastic. I was glad when you split up." Alice bit into a piece of bread. "Who are you seeing now? Some married woman, I bet."

"Why would you think that?"

"We haven't met anyone since Monique. So. You must have somebody under wraps. The Dark Lady."

"I wish you wouldn't try to act sophisticated," he said. "Do you really think I'm conducting some great love affair?"

"I figured you must have somebody." She sounded bored. She was studying his face. "Boy, those guys really did a job on you, didn't they?"

Wiley moved his plate to one side. "There was just one," he said. "Short fellow. No bigger than a minute."

"Mac told me two. 'Two of our dusky brethren' was what he said. Where did he get that stuff?"

"From me," Wiley said.

And then, because he trusted her and felt the need, he

began to tell her what had really happened to him the night before. Alice listened without any disgust or pity that he could see. She seemed purely interested. Now and then she laughed, because in talking about it Wiley couldn't help but make his little disaster into a story, and telling stories, even those about loneliness and humiliation, naturally brought out the hambone and wag in him. He could see she was having a good time listening to him, that this wasn't what she'd expected when Mac asked her to look in on him. And she was hearing some straight talk. She didn't get that at home. Mac was good-hearted, but he was also a tomcat and a liar.

Wiley's way of telling stories about himself was to tell them as if they'd happened to someone else. And from that distance he could see that there was something to be laughed at in the spectacle of a man who energetically professed the examined life, the life of the spirit and the mind, getting drunk and brawling over strange women. Well, the body had a mind of its own. He told it like that, like his body had abducted him for its own low purposes, like he'd been lashed to the back of a foaming runaway horse hellbent on dragging him through every degradation.

But it was not in the end a funny story. When he told Alice what went on in his class that morning she grew watchful and grave.

"I was speechless," he said. "I couldn't say a thing. We do *Native Son*, we do *Invisible Man*. I get them really talking, really thinking about all this stuff, and then I start a race riot in my own classroom."

"Maybe you should tell them the truth."

"Are you serious?"

"They'd respect you for it."

"Hah!"

"Well, they should."

"Come on, Alice."

"Some of them would. And they'd be the right ones."

"It would get all over school. I'd get fired."

"That's true," Alice said. She rested her cheek on her hand. "But still."

"Still what?" When she didn't answer, he said, "All right, let's say I don't care about getting fired. I do, but let's just hypothetically say I go in there tomorrow and tell them everything, the works. You know what they'll think? They'll think I'm making it up—the second story, not the first. You know, out of bleeding-heart sentimentality, to make the black kids feel better. But what'll really happen, they'll end up feeling even worse. Condescended to. Insulted. They'll think I'm lying to protect them, as if they were guilty of something. Everyone will think I'm lying."

Wiley could see her hesitate. Then she said, "But you won't be lying. You'll be telling the truth."

"Yes, but no one will know it!"

"You will. You'll know it."

"Look. Alice." Wiley was angry now, and impatient. He waited, and then spoke so that his anger would not show. He said, "I feel terrible. I can't even count all the things I've done wrong today. But I did them, they're done. Trying to undo them will only make things worse, and not just for me. For those kids." This seemed logical to Wiley, well and reasonably said.

"Maybe so." She was turning one of her rings nervously. "Maybe I'm being simplistic, but I just don't see where telling the truth can be wrong. I always thought that's what you were there for."

Wiley had other arguments to make. That he was a teacher, and could not afford to gamble with his moral authority. That when the truth did more harm than a lie, you had to give the lie its due. That if other people had to suffer just so you could have a clean conscience you should accept your fallen condition and get on with it. They were good arguments, the very oil of adult life, but he said nothing. He was no fool, he knew what her answers would be, because after all they were his answers too. He simply couldn't act on them.

"Alice," he said. "Are you listening?"

She nodded.

"I shouldn't have dropped all this stuff on you. It's too confusing."

"I'm not confused."

He didn't answer.

"I have to go," she said.

He walked her to the door.

"I won't say anything to Mac," she told him.

"I know that. I trust you."

"To do what? Keep secrets from my husband?" She laughed, not pleasantly. "Don't worry," she said. "I know how he is."

Wiley corrected essays the rest of the afternoon. He broke for dinner and then finished them off. It was a good batch, the best he'd had all year. They were on "Bartleby the Scrivener." One of his students, a girl, had compared the situation to a marriage, with Bartleby as the wife and the narrator as the husband: "He looks at Bartleby the way men look at women, as if Bartleby has no other purpose on earth than to be of use to him." She bent the story around to fit her argument, but Wiley didn't mind. The essay was fresh and passionate. This particular girl wouldn't have thought to take such a view at the beginning of the year. Wiley was moved, and proud of her.

He recorded the grades in his book and then called the Filbert Street number of Dr. K. P. Newman. When she answered, he said, "It's me, Kathleen. From last night," he added.

"You," she said. "Where did you get my number?"

"Out of the phone book. I just wanted to set things straight."

"You called me before, didn't you?" she said. "You called me at work."

"Yes."

"I knew it. You didn't even say anything. You didn't even have the balls to give your own name."

"That was a joke," Wiley said.

"You're crazy. You call me again and I'll have the police on you."

"Wait. Kathleen. I need to see you."

"I don't need to see you."

"Wait. Please, listen. I'm not like that, not like I seemed last night. Really, Kathleen. Last night was a series of misunderstandings. I just want to stop by for a minute or two, straighten everything out."

"What, you have my *address*?"

"It's in the book."

"Christ! I can't believe this! Don't even think about coming here. Mike's here," she said, "and this time I won't stop him. I mean it."

"You aren't married to Mike."

"Who said?"

"You would've said if you were."

"So? What difference does it make?"

"It makes a difference."

"You're crazy."

"All I need is a few minutes to talk things over."

"I'm hanging up."

"Just a few minutes, Kathleen. That's all I'm asking. Then I'll leave, if you still want me to."

"Mike's here," she said. She was silent. Then, just before she hung up, she said, "Don't you ever call me at work again."

Wiley liked the sound of that; it meant she assumed a future for them.

Before going out he looked himself over in the mirror. He wasn't pretty, but he could still talk. All he had to do was get her to listen. He'd keep saying her name. *Kathleen.* Say it in that moony broguish way she liked. Said that way, almost sung, her name had power over her; he had seen it last night, the willing girl blooming on the face of the woman, the girl ready for love. He would hit that note, and once he got her listening there was no telling what might happen, because all he really needed was words, and of words, Wiley knew, there was no end.

Flyboys

M y friend Clark and I decided to build a jet plane. We spent weeks perfecting our design at the draftsman's table in his bedroom. Sometimes Clark let me put on the green eyeshade and wield the compasses and calipers, but never for long. I drew like a lip-reader reads; watching me was torture for him. When he couldn't take it anymore he'd bump me aside, leaving me free to fool with his things—the samurai sword, the Webley pistol with the plugged barrel—and wander the house.

Clark's mom was usually out somewhere. I formed the habit of making myself a sandwich and settling back in the leather chair in the den, where I listened to old records and studied the family photo albums. They were lucky people, Clark's parents, lucky and unsurprised by their luck. You could see in the pictures that they took it all in stride, the big spreads behind them, the boats and cars, and their relaxed, handsome families who, it was clear, did not get laid off, or come down with migraines, or lock each other out of the house. I pondered each picture as if it were a door I might enter, until something turned in me and I grew irritable. Then I put the albums away, and went back to Clark's room to inspect his work and demand revisions.

Sure and commanding in everything but this, Clark took most of my ideas to heart, which made a tyrant of me. The more attentive he was, the more I bullied him. His own proposals I laughed off as moronic jokes. Clark cared more for the perfection of the plane than for his own vanity; he thought nothing of crumpling a page he'd spent hours on and starting over because of some brainstorm I'd had. This wasn't humility, but an assurance that ran to imperturbable depths and rendered him deaf to any appeal when he rejected one of my inspirations. There were times—many times—when I contemplated that squarish head of his as I hefted the samurai sword, and imagined the stroke that would drop it to the floor like a ripe melon.

Clark was stubborn but there was no meanness in him. He wouldn't turn on you; he was the same one day as the next, earnest and practical. Though the family had money and spent it freely, he wasn't spoiled or interested in possessions except as instruments of his projects. In the eight or nine months we'd been friends we had shot two horror movies with his dad's 8-mm. camera, built a catapult that worked so well his parents made us take it apart, and fashioned a monstrous, unsteerable sled out of a bedframe and five wooden skis we found in his neighbor's trash. We also wrote a radio mystery for a competition one of the local stations put on every year, Clark patiently retyping the script as I improvised more tortuous plot twists and highfalutin dialogue ("My dear Carstairs, it was really most astute of you to notice the mud on my smoking jacket. How unfortunate that you failed to decry the derringer in my pocket!"). We were flabbergasted that we didn't win.

I supplied the genius, or so I believed. But I understood even then that Clark gave it form and did all the work. His drawings of our plane were crisp and minutely detailed, like real blueprints that a spy would cut somebody's throat for. As I pondered them at the end of the day (frontal and side views, views from above and behind and below), the separate designs locked together like a puzzle and lifted away from the flatness of the page. They became an airplane, a jet—my jet. And through all the long run home I was in the cockpit of my jet, skimming sawtooth peaks, weaving through steep valleys, buzzing fishermen in the sound and tearing over the city in such a storm of flash and thunder that football games stopped in mid-play, cheerleaders gaping up at me, legs still flexed under their plaid skirts. A barrel roll, a waggle of the wings and I was gone, racing up through the clouds. I could feel the Gs in my arms, my chest, my face. The skin pulled back from my cheeks. Tears streaked from my eyes. The plane shook like crazy. When I couldn't go any higher, I went higher. Sweet Jesus, I did some flying!

Clark and I hadn't talked much about the actual construction of the jet. We let that question hang while we finetuned the plans. But the plans couldn't be worked on forever; we were getting bored and stale. And then Clark came up to me at recess one day and said he knew where we could get a canopy. When I asked him where, he looked over at the guy I'd been shooting baskets with and pushed his lips together. Clark had long ago decided that I was a security risk. "You'll see," he said, and walked off.

All afternoon I nagged him to tell me where the canopy was, who we were getting it from. He wouldn't say a thing. I wanted to tear him apart.

Instead of heading toward his place after school, Clark led me down the avenue past the post office and Safeway and the line of drive-ins and pinball joints where the high-school kids hung out. Clark had long legs and never looked to right or left, he just flat-out marched, so I had to hustle to keep up. I resented being at his heels, sweaty and short of breath and ignorant of our destination, and most of all I resented his knowing that I would follow him anyway.

We turned down the alley beside the Odd Fellows hall and skirted a big lot full of school buses, then cut through a construction site that gave onto a park where I'd once been chased by some older boys. On the other side of the park we crossed the bridge over Flint Creek, swollen with a week's heavy rain. Beyond the bridge the road turned into a series of mudholes bordered by small, soggy-looking houses overhung by dripping trees. By then I'd stopped asking where we were going, because I knew. I had been this way before, many times.

"I don't remember Freddy having any airplane canopies around," I said.

"He's got a whole barnful of stuff."

"I know, I've seen it, but I didn't see any canopies."

"Maybe he just got it."

"That's a big fat maybe."

Clark picked up the pace.

I said, "So, Mr. Top Secret, how come you told Freddy about the plane?"

"I didn't. Sandra told him."

I let that ride, since I'd told Sandra.

Freddy lived at the dead end of the street. As Clark and I got closer I could hear the snarl of a chain saw from the woods behind the house. Freddy and I used to lose ourselves all day in there. I hung back while Clark went up to the house and knocked. Freddy's mother opened the door. She let Clark in and waited as I crossed the yard and mounted the steps. "Well, aren't you a sight for sore eyes," she said, not as a reproach, though I felt it that way. She ruffled my hair as I went past. "You've grown a few inches."

"Yes, ma'am."

"Freddy's in the kitchen."

Freddy closed his book and stood up from the table. He

smiled shyly. "Hi," he said, and I said "Hi" back. It came hard. We hadn't spoken in almost a year, since he went into the hospital. Freddy's mother came in behind us and said, "Sit down, boys. Take off your coats. Freddy, put some of those cookies on a plate."

"I can't stay long," Clark said, but nobody answered him and he finally hung his jacket on a chair and pulled up to the table. It was a round table that took up most of the kitchen. Freddy's brother, Tanker, had carved pictures all over the tabletop, *Field and Stream*-type depictions of noble stags and leaping fish, eagles with rabbits in their talons, cougars crouched above mountain goats. He always kept his Barlow knife busy while he drank Olympia and told his stories. Like the stories, the pictures all ran together. They would've covered the whole table by now if Tanker hadn't been killed.

The air smelled like laundry, and the windows were misted up. Freddy shook some Oreos onto a plate and handed it to me. I passed it on to Clark without taking any. The plate was dingy. Not encrusted, no major food groups in evidence—just dingy. Business as usual. I never ate at Freddy's unless I was starving. Clark didn't seem to notice. He grabbed a handful, and after a show of indecision Freddy's mother took one. She was a thin woman with shoulder blades that stuck out like wings when she hunched over, as she did now, nibbling at her Oreo. She turned to me, her eyes so sad I had to force myself not to look away. "I can't get over how you've grown," she said. "Freddy, hasn't he grown?"

"Like a weed," Freddy said.

"By leaps and bounds," I said, falling into our old game in spite of myself.

Clark looked back and forth between us.

Freddy's mother said, "I understand you boys are building an airplane."

"We're just getting started," Clark said.

"Well, that's just wonderful," Freddy's mother said. "An airplane. Think of that."

"Right now we're looking for a canopy," Clark said.

Nobody spoke for a while. Freddy's mother crossed her arms over her chest and bent down even farther. Then she said, "Freddy, you should tell your friends what you were telling me about that fellow in your book."

"That's okay," Freddy said. "Maybe later."

"About the mountains of skulls."

"Human skulls?" I said.

"Mountains of them," Freddy's mother said.

"Tamerlane," Freddy said. And without further delay he began to describe Tamerlane's revenge on the Persian cities that had resisted his progress. It was grisly stuff, but he did not scrimp on details or try to hide his pleasure in them, or in the starchy phrases he'd picked up from whatever book he was reading. That was Freddy for you. Gentle as a lamb, but very big on the Vikings and Aztecs and Genghis Khan and the Crusaders, all the great old disembowelers and eyeball-gougers. So was I. It was an interest we shared. Clark listened, looking a little stunned.

I never found out exactly how Tanker got killed; it was a motorcycle accident outside Spokane, that was all Freddy told me. You had to know Tanker to know what that meant. This was a very unlucky family. Bats took over their attic. Their cars laid transmissions like eggs. They got caught switching license plates and dumping garbage illegally and owing back taxes, or at least Ivan did. Ivan was Freddy's stepfather and a world of bad luck all by himself. He wasn't vicious or evil, but full of cute ideas that got him in trouble and made things even worse than they already were, like not paying property taxes on the basis of some veterans' exemption he'd heard about but didn't bother to read up on, and that turned out not to apply to him. That brilliant stroke almost cost them the house, which Freddy's father had left free and clear when he died. Tanker was the only one in the family who could stand up to Ivan, and not just because he was bigger and more competent. Ivan had a soft spot for him. After the accident he took to his bed for almost a week straight, then vanished.

When Tanker was home everybody'd be in the kitchen, sitting around the table and cracking up at his stories. He told stories about himself that I would've locked away for good, like the time his bike broke down in the middle of nowhere and a car stopped but instead of giving him a lift the guys inside hit him over the head with a lunch bag full of fresh shit. Then a patrolman arrested him and made him ride to the station in his trunk—all in the middle of a snowstorm. Tanker told that story as if it was the most precious thing that ever happened to him, tears glistening in his eyes. He had lots of friends, wise guys in creaking leather jackets, and he filled the house with them. He could fix anything—plumbing, engines, leaky roofs, you name it. He took Freddy and me on fishing trips in his rattletrap truck, and gave us Indian names. I was Hard-to-Camp-With, because I complained and snored. Freddy was Cheap-to-Feed.

After Tanker got killed everything changed at Freddy's. The house had the frozen, echoey quiet of abandonment. Ivan finally came back from wherever he'd disappeared to, but he spent most of his time away on some new enterprise. When Freddy and I got to the house after school it was always dim and still. His mother kept to herself in the back bedroom. Sometimes she came out to offer us a sandwich and ask us questions about our day, but I wished she wouldn't. I had never seen such sorrow; it appalled me. And I was even more appalled by her attempts to overcome it, because they so plainly, pathetically failed, and in failing opened up the view of a world I had only begun to suspect, where wounds did not heal, and things did not work out for the best.

One day Freddy and I were shooting baskets in the driveway when his mother called him inside. We'd been playing horse, and I took advantage of his absence to practice my hook shot. My hook had Freddy jinxed; he couldn't even hit the backboard with it. I dribbled and shot, dribbled and shot, ten, twenty times; fifty times. Freddy still didn't come back. It was very quiet. The only sound was the ball hitting the backboard, the rim, the asphalt. I stopped shooting after a while and stood there, waiting, bouncing the ball. The ball was overinflated and rose fast to the hand, making a hollow whang shadowed by a high ringing note that lingered in the silence. It began to give me the creeps. But I kept bouncing the ball, somehow unable to break the rhythm I'd fallen into. My hand moved by itself, lightly palming the pebbled skin and pushing the ball down just hard enough to bring it back. The sound grew louder and larger and emptier, the sound of emptiness itself, emptiness throbbing like a headache. Spooked, I caught the ball and held it. I looked at the house. Nothing moved there. I thought of the woman closed up inside, and Freddy, closed up with her, swallowed by misery. In its stillness the house seemed conscious, expectant. It seemed to be waiting. I put the ball down and walked to the end of the driveway, then broke into a run. I was still running when I reached the park. That was the day the older boys chased me, their blood roused by the spectacle of my rabbity flight. They kept after me for a hundred yards or so and then fell back, though they could've caught me if they'd had their hearts in it. But they were running for sport; the seriousness of my panic confused them, put them off their stride.

Such panic . . . where did it come from? It couldn't have been just the situation at Freddy's. The shakiness of my own family was becoming more and more apparent. At the time I didn't admit to this knowledge, not for a moment, but it was always there, waiting in the gut: a sourness of foreboding, a cramp of alarm at any sign of misfortune or weakness in others, as if such things were catching.

Freddy had asthma. Not long after I ran away from his house he suffered a severe attack and went into the hospital. Our teacher told the class about it. She had everyone write get-well notes, and handed out mimeographed sheets with the address of the hospital and the visiting hours. It was an easy walk. I knew I should go, and I thought about it so much that whatever else I did that week seemed mainly to be *not going*, but I couldn't make myself do it. When Freddy came back to school I was unable to speak to him or even face him. I went straight home after the bell rang, using the main entrance instead of the side door where we used to meet. And then I saw that he was avoiding me, too. He ate at the opposite end of the cafeteria; when we passed in the hallway he blushed and stared at the floor. He acted as if he had done me some wrong, and the shame I felt at this made me even more skittish. I was very lonely for a time, then Clark and I became friends. This was my first visit to Freddy's since the day I bolted.

Clark worked his way through the Oreos as Freddy told his gruesome tale, and when he came to the end I started one of my own from a book my brother had given me about Quantrill's Raiders. It was a truly terrible story, a cruel, mortifying story—the star sociopath was a man named "Bloody Bill." I was aware of Freddy watching me with something like rapture. Freddy's mother shook her head when the going got rough and made exclamations of shock and dismay—"No! He never!"—just like she used to do back when the three of us watched "Queen for a Day" every afternoon, drooling shamelessly over the weird, woeful narratives sobbed out by the competing wretches. Clark watched me without joy. He was impatient for business, and too sane for all this ghoulish stuff. I knew that he was seeing me in a different way, a way he probably didn't like, but I kept piling it on. I couldn't let go of the old pleasure, almost forgotten, of having Freddy on my hook, and feeling his own pleasure thrumming through the line.

And then the back door swung open and Ivan leaned his head into the kitchen. His face was even bigger and whiter than I remembered, and as if to confirm my memory he wore a red hunting cap that was too small and sat his head like a party hat. Black mud encased his pant legs almost to his knees. He looked at me and said, "Hey, by gum! Long time no see!" One of the lenses of his spectacles had a daub of mud in the middle, like an eyeball on a pair of joke glasses. He looked at Clark, then at Freddy's mother. "Hon, you aren't gonna believe this—that darn truck got stuck again."

A damp wind was blowing. Freddy and Clark and I stood with shoulders hunched, hands in our pockets, and looked on as Ivan circled Tanker's old pickup and explained why it wasn't his fault the tires were mired almost to the axle. "The truth is, the old gal just can't pull her weight anymore." He gave the fender a rub. "Past her prime—has been for years."

"Yessir," Freddy said. "She's long in the tooth and that's a fact."

"There you go," Ivan said.

"Ready for the pasture," I said.

"Over the hill," Freddy said.

"That's it exactly," Ivan said. "I just can't bring myself to sell her." And then his jaw started quaking and I thought with horror that he was about to cry. But he didn't. He caught his lower lip under his teeth, sucked it musingly, and pushed it out again. His lips were full and expressive. I tended to watch them for signs of mood rather than his eyes, which he kept buried in a cunning squint.

"So. Gotta get the wood out. You fellows ready to use some of those muscles?"

Freddy and I looked at each other.

Clark was staring at the truck. "You want us to unload all of that?"

"Won't take an hour, strapping boys like you," Ivan said. "Maybe an hour by the time you load her up again," he added.

The truck bed was filled with logs, stacked as high as the sides and heaped to a peak in the middle. Ivan had been clearing out the woods behind the house. Most of it was gone by now, nearly an acre of trees turned into a stumpy bog crisscrossed by tire ruts filled with black water. Behind the bog stood the house of a family whose pale, stringy daughters quarreled incessantly with their mother, screaming as they ran out the door, screaming as they jumped into the souped-up cars of their boyfriends. The father and son also drove hot rods, maintaining them on parts cannibalized from the collection of wrecks in their backyard. They came out during the afternoons and weekends to crawl under the cars and shout at each other over the clanging of their wrenches. Freddy and I used to spy on the family from the trees, our faces darkened, twigs stuck in our hair. He wouldn't have to steal up on them now; they'd be in plain view all the time.

Ivan had been hard at work, turning trees into firewood. Firewood was cheap. Whatever he got wouldn't be worth it, worth all the green and the birds and the scolding squirrels, the coolness in summer, the long shafts of afternoon light. This place had been Iroquois wilderness to me, English forest and African jungle. It had been Mars. Gone, all of them. I was a boy who didn't know he would never build a jet, but I knew that this lake of mud was the work of a fool.

"I'll bet you can drive it out without unloading," Clark said.

"Already tried." Ivan lowered himself onto a stump and looked around with a satisfied air. "Sooner you fellows get started, sooner you'll be done."

"A stitch in time saves nine," I said.

"No time like the present," Freddy said.

"There you go," Ivan said.

Clark had been standing on a web of roots. He stepped off and walked toward the truck. As he got closer the ground turned soupy and he went up on tiptoe, then began hopping from foot to foot, but there was no firm place to land and every time he jumped he went in deeper. When he sank past his ankles he gave up and mucked ahead, his sneakers slurping, picking up more goop with each step. By the time he reached the truck they looked like medicine balls. He crouched by one rear tire, then the other.

"We can put down corduroy tracks," he said.

Ivan winked in our direction. "Corduroy tracks, you say!"

"That's what they used to do when covered wagons got stuck," Clark said. "Put logs down."

"Son, does that look like a covered wagon to you?"

"Also artillery pieces. In the Civil War."

"Maybe we should just unload the truck," I said.

"Hold your horses." Ivan put his hands on his knees. He studied Clark. "I like a boy with ideas," he said. "Go on, give it a stab."

"Never hurts to try," Freddy said.

"That's it exactly," Ivan said.

Freddy and I walked up to the barn for a couple of shovels. We cut wide of the ruts and puddles but the mud

still sucked at our shoes. Once we were alone, I kept thinking how thin he'd gotten. I couldn't come up with anything
to say. He didn't speak either.

I waited while Freddy went into the barn, and when he
came back outside I said, "We're going to move." No one
had told me any such thing, but those words came to mind
and it felt right to say them.

Freddy handed me a shovel. "Where to?"

"I don't know."

"When."

"I'm not sure."

We started back.

"I hope you don't move," Freddy said.

"Maybe we won't," I said. "Maybe we'll end up stay-
ing."

"That would be great, if you stayed."

"There's no place like home."

"Home is where the heart is," Freddy said, but he was
looking at the ground just ahead of him and didn't smile
back at me.

We took turns digging out the wheels, one resting while
the other two worked. Ivan laughed whenever we slipped
into the mud, but otherwise watched in silence. It was impossible to dig and keep your feet, especially as we got
deeper. Finally I gave up and knelt as I worked—you had
more leverage that way—and Clark and Freddy followed
suit. I was sheathed in mud up to my waist and elbows. My
condition was hopeless, so I stopped trying to spare myself
and just let go. I surrendered to the spirit of the mud. It's
fair to say I wallowed.

What we did, under Clark's direction, was cut a wide
trench from the bottom of each tire forward about five feet,
sloping up like a ramp. We jammed cordwood under the
tires and then lined the ramps with more logs as we dug.
We were about finished when the walls started to collapse.

Clark took it personally. "Fudge!" he kept saying, and Ivan laughed and swayed back and forth on the stump. Clark yelled at Freddy and me to *dig! dig! dig!* and stretched flat on his stomach and scooped the sliding mud out with his hands. I could hear Freddy laboring for breath, but he didn't let up, and neither did I. We burrowed like moles and then came a moment when the tracks were clear and the walls holding, and Clark told Ivan to move the truck. Clark was excited and barked at him as he'd been barking at us. Ivan sat there blinking. Clark pitched some spare logs back into the truck. "Come on, guys," he said. "We'll push."

Ivan stood and brushed off his hands and walked over to the truck, still watching Clark. Before he climbed into the cab, he said, "Young fellow, if you ever need a job, call me."

Clark and Freddy and I braced ourselves against the tailgate as Ivan cranked the engine and put it in gear. The rear wheels started to spin, churning back geysers of mud. I was in the middle so I didn't catch much of it, but Freddy and Clark got plastered. Freddy turned away and then leaned forward again and started pushing with Clark and me. Ivan was rocking the truck to and fro, trying to get it onto the logs. It rose a little, hesitated, then slipped and spewed back another blast of mud. Clark and Freddy looked like they'd been stuccoed. They moved in closer beside me as Ivan got the truck rocking again. I held my breath against the heavy black exhaust. My eyes burned. The truck rocked and rose again, hung on the lip. Clark grunted, again and again and again. I picked up his rhythm and pushed for all I was worth, and then my feet slid and I fell flat out as the truck jerked forward. The tires screamed on the wood. A log shot back and flipped past Clark's head. He didn't seem to notice. He was watching the truck. It gathered speed on the track we'd made and hit the mud again and somehow slithered on, languidly, noisily, rear end sashaying, two great plumes of mud arcing off the back wheels. The wheels spun wildly, the engine shrieked, logs tumbled off the sides. The truck slewed and swayed across the bog and rose abruptly, shedding skirts of mud, as it gained the broken asphalt in front of the barn. Ivan shifted gears, beeped merrily, and drove away.

"You all right?" Clark said.

Freddy was bent double, head almost between his knees. He held up a hand but went on panting. The truck had left behind an exaggerated silence in which I could hear the clutch and rasp of every breath he took. It sounded like hard work, hard and lonely. When I moved toward him he waved me off. Clark picked up a stick and began scraping his sneakers. This seemed an optimistic project, caked as he was to the eyeballs, but he went about it with method and gravity. Freddy straightened up. His face was pallid, his chest rose and fell like a bird's. He stood there a while, watching Clark wield the stick. "We can get cleaned up at the house," he said.

"If it's okay with you," Clark said, "I'd like to take a look at that canopy."

I'd been hoping all afternoon that Clark would drop the subject of the canopy, because I knew as a matter of absolute fact that Freddy didn't have one. But he did. It was in the loft of the barn, where Freddy's father had stored items of special interest from the salvage yard he'd owned. In all the rainy afternoons we'd spent fooling around up there I must have seen it a hundred times, but having no use for it, not even recognizing what it was, I'd never taken note. The canopy was smaller than our plans specified, but the plans could be changed; this was the genuine article. Freddy played the flashlight slowly up and down the length of it. He must have prepared for this moment, because unlike everything else up there the canopy was free of dust—polished, even, from the look of it. The light picked up a few scratches. Otherwise it was perfect: clear, unbroken, complete with flashing. Simple, but technical too. Real.

If I'd had any doubts, they left me. It was obvious that our jet was not only possible but as good as built. All we had to do was keep having days like this and soon the pieces would all come together, and we'd be flying.

Clark asked Freddy what he wanted for it.

"Nothing. It's just sitting here."

We poked around a while and went back to the house, where Freddy's mother declared shock at our condition and ordered us to strip and hose off. Clark wouldn't do it, he just washed his face and hands, but I took a long shower and then Freddy's mother gave me some of Tanker's clothes to wear home and wrapped my own dismal duds in a butcher-paper parcel tied off with a string handle, like a mess of gizzards. Freddy walked us to the end of the street. The light was failing. I looked back once and saw him still standing there. When I looked again he was gone.

We stopped on the bridge over Flint Creek and threw rocks at a bottle caught in some weeds. I was all pumped up from getting the truck out and seeing the canopy, plus Freddy's mother had lent me Tanker's motorcycle jacket, which, though it hung to my fingertips, filled me with a conviction of my own powers that verged on madness. I was half hoping we'd run into those older boys in the park so I could whip their asses for them.

I leaned over the railing, spat into the water.

"Freddy wants in," Clark said.

"He said that? He didn't tell me."

"You were in the shower."

"So what did he say?"

"Just that he wished he could come in with us, on the plane."

"What, or he takes the canopy back?"

"No. He just asked."

"We'd have to redesign the whole cockpit. It would change everything."

Clark had a rock in his hand. He looked at it with some interest, then flipped it into the creek.

"What did you tell him?"

"I said we'd let him know."

"What do you think?"

"He seems okay. You know him better than I do."

"Freddy's great, it's just . . ."

Clark waited for me to finish. When it was clear that I wasn't going to, he said, "Whatever you want."

I told him that all things considered, I'd just as soon keep it to the two of us.

As we crossed the park he asked me to have dinner at his place so he wouldn't get skinned alive about the clothes. His dad was still in Portland, he said, as if that explained something. Clark took his time on the walk home, looking in shop windows and inspecting cars in the lots we passed. When we finally got to the house it was all lit up and music was playing. Even with the windows closed we could hear strains of it from the bottom of the sidewalk. Clark stopped. He stood there, listening.

"Strauss," he said. "Good. She's happy."

Sanity

Getting from La Jolla to Alta Vista State Hospital isn't easy, unless you have a car or a breakdown. April's father had a breakdown and they got him out there in no time at all. The trip took longer for April and her stepmother; they had to catch two different buses, hike up a hot winding road through the hospital grounds, then walk back down to the bus stop when the visit was over. There were few drivers on the road, and none stopped to offer a lift. April didn't blame them. They probably figured she and Claire were patients out for a stroll. That's what she would've thought, coming upon the two of them out here. One look and she would have kept going.

Claire was tall and erect. She was wearing a smart gray suit and high heels and a wide-brimmed black hat. She carried herself a little stiffly because of the heels but kept up a purposeful, dignified pace. "Ship of State"—that was what April's father called Claire when she felt summoned to a demonstration of steadiness and resolve. April followed along in loose order. She stopped now and then to catch her breath and let some distance open up between them, then hurried to close that distance. April was a short muscular girl with a mannish stride. She was scowling in the hazy midsummer light. Her hands were red. She had on a sleeveless dress, yellow with black flowers, that she knew to be ugly and wore anyway because it made people conscious of her.

Two cars went by, their tires moving over the tacky asphalt with the sound of tape being peeled. April's father had sold the Volkswagen for almost nothing a few days before he went into the hospital, and Claire wouldn't even look at anything else. She had some money in the bank, but she was saving it for a trip to Italy with her sister when April's father came home.

Claire had been quiet through most of the visit, quiet and on edge, and now that it was over she did not try to hide her relief. She wanted to talk. She said that the doctor they'd spoken with reminded her of Walt Darsh, her husband during the last ice age. That was how she located whatever had happened to her in the past—"during the last ice age." April knew she wanted to be told that she still looked good, and it wouldn't have been a lie to say so, but this time April said nothing.

She had heard about Walt Darsh before, his faithlessness and cruelty. Though the stories Claire told were interesting, they left April troubled, strange to herself. As soon as Claire got started, April said, "If he was so bad, how come you married him?"

Claire didn't answer right away. She walked more slowly, and inclined her long neck thoughtfully, and gave every sign of being occupied with a new and demanding question. She looked at April, then looked away. "Sex," she said.

April could see the glitter of windshields in the distance. There was a bench at the bus stop; when they got there she was going to lie down and close her eyes and pretend to sleep.

"It's hard to explain," Claire said cautiously, as if April had pressed her. "It wasn't his looks. Darsh isn't really what you'd call handsome. He has a sly, pointy kind of face . . . like a fox. You know what I mean? It isn't just the shape, it's the way he watches you, always grinning a little, like he's got the goods on you." Claire stopped in the shade of a tree. She took off her hat, smoothed back her hair, curled some loose strands behind her ears, then put her hat back on and set it just so across her forehead. She found a Kleenex in her purse and dabbed the corner of one eye where a thin line of mascara had run. Claire had the gift, mysterious to April, of knowing what she looked like even without a mirror. April's face was always a surprise to her, always somehow different than she'd imagined it.

"Of course, that can be attractive too," Claire said, "being looked at in that way. With most men it's annoying, but not always. With Darsh it was attractive. So I suppose you could say that it *was* his looks, in the literal sense. If you see the distinction."

April saw the distinction, also Claire's pleasure in having made it. She was unhappy with this line of talk but couldn't do anything about it, because it was her own fault that Claire believed she was ripe for unrestrained discussion of these matters. Over the last few months Claire had decided that April was sleeping with Stuart, the boy she went out with. This was not the case. Stuart dropped hints now and then in his polite, witty, hopeless way, but he wasn't really serious and neither was April. She hadn't told Claire the truth because in the beginning it gave her satisfaction to be seen as a woman of experience. Claire was a snob about knowing the ways of the world; it pleased April to crowd her turf a little. Claire never asked, she simply assumed, and once that assumption took hold there was no way to straighten things out.

The brim of Claire's hat waved up and down. She

seemed to be having an idea she agreed with. "Looks are part of it," she said, "definitely. But not the whole story. It never is, with sex, is it?—just one thing. Like technique, for instance." Claire turned and started down the road again, head still pensively bent. April could feel a lecture coming. Claire taught sociology at the same junior college where April's father used to teach psych, and like him she was quick to mount the podium.

"People write about technique," she said, "as if it's the whole ball game, which is a complete joke. You know who's really getting off on technique? Publishers, that's who. Because they can turn it into a commodity. They can merchandise it as know-how, like traveling in Mexico or building a redwood deck. The only problem is, it doesn't work. You know why? It turns sex into a literary experience."

April couldn't stop herself from giggling. This made her sound foolish, as she knew.

"I'm serious," Claire said. "You can tell right away that it's coming out of some book. You start seeing yourself in one of those little squiggly drawings, with your zones all marked out and some earnest little cartoon guy working his way through them, being really considerate."

Claire stopped again and gazed out over the fields that lined the road, one hand resting in a friendly way on top of a fence post. Back in the old days, according to April's father, the patients used to raise things in these fields. Now they were overgrown with scrubby trees and tall yellow grass. Insects shrilled loudly.

"That's another reason those books are worthless," Claire said. "They're all about sharing, being tender, anticipating your partner's needs, etcetera etcetera. It's like Sunday school in bed. I'm not kidding, April. That's what it's all about, all this technique stuff. Judeo-Christian conscientiousness. The Golden Rule. You know what I mean?"

"I guess," April said.

"We're talking about a very basic transaction," Claire said. "A lot more basic than lending money to a friend. Think about it. Lending is a highly evolved activity. Other species don't do it, only us. Just look at all the things that go into lending money. Social stability, trust, generosity. Imagining yourself in the other person's place. It's incredibly advanced, incredibly civilized. I'm all for it. My point is, sex comes from another place. Sex isn't civilized. It isn't about being unselfish."

An ambulance went slowly past. April looked after it, then back at Claire, who was still staring out over the fields. April saw the line of her profile in the shadow of the hat, saw how dry and cool her skin was, the composure of her smile. April saw these things and felt her own sticky, worried, incomplete condition. "We ought to get going," she said.

"To tell the truth," Claire said, "that was one of the things that attracted me to Darsh. He was totally selfish, totally out to please himself. That gave him a certain heat. A certain power. The libbers would kill me for saying this, but it's true. Did I ever tell you about our honeymoon?"

"No." April made her voice flat and grudging, though she was curious.

"Or the maid thing? Did I ever tell you about Darsh's maid thing?"

"No," April said again. "What about the honeymoon?"

Claire said, "That's a long story. I'll tell you about the maid thing."

"You don't have to tell me anything," April said.

Claire went on smiling to herself. "Back when Darsh was a kid, his mother took him on a trip to Europe. The grand tour. He was too young for it, thirteen, fourteen—that age. By the time they got to Amsterdam he was sick of museums, he never wanted to see another painting in his life. That's the trouble with pushing culture at children, they end up hating it. It's better to let them come to it on their own, don't you think?"

April shrugged.

"Take Jane Austen, for example. They were shoving Jane Austen down my throat when I was in the eighth grade. *Pride and Prejudice.* Of course I absolutely loathed it, because I couldn't see what was really going on, the sexual play behind the manners, the social critique, the *economics.* I hadn't lived. You have to have some life under your belt before you can make any sense of a book like that.

"Anyway, Darsh dug in his heels when they got to Amsterdam. He wouldn't budge. He stayed in the hotel room all day long, reading mysteries and ordering stuff from room service, while his mother went out and looked at paintings. One afternoon a maid came up to the room to polish the chandelier. She had a stepladder, and from where Darsh was sitting he couldn't help seeing up her dress. All the way up, okay? And she knew it. He knew she knew, because after a while he didn't even try to hide it, he just stared. She didn't say a word. Not one. She took her sweet time up there too, polishing every pendant, cool as a cucumber. Darsh said it went on for a couple of hours, which means maybe half an hour—which is a pretty long time, if you think about it."

"Then what happened?"

"Nothing. Nothing happened. That's the whole point, April. If something had happened it would've broken the spell. It would have let out all that incredible energy. But it stayed locked in. It's always there, boiling away at this insane fourteen-year-old level, just waiting to explode. Maids are one of Darsh's real hot spots. He used to own the whole outfit, probably still does—you know, frilly white blouse, black skirt, black nylons with all the little snaps. It's a cliché, of course. Pornographers have been using it for a hundred years. But so what. It still works. Most of our desires are clichés, right? Ready to wear, one size fits all. I doubt if it's even possible to have an original desire anymore."

"He actually made you wear that stuff?"

April saw Claire freeze at her words, as if she'd said something hurtful and low. Claire straightened up and slowly started walking again. April hung back, then followed a few steps behind until Claire waited for her to catch up. After a time Claire said, "No, dear. He didn't make me do anything. It's exciting when somebody wants something that much. I loved the way he looked at me. Like he wanted to eat me alive, but innocent too.

"Maybe it sounds cheap. It's hard to describe."

Claire was quiet then, and so was April. She did not feel any need for description. She thought she could imagine the look Darsh had given Claire, in fact she could see it perfectly, though no one had ever looked at her that way. Certainly not Stuart. She felt safe with him, safe and sleepy. Nobody like Stuart would ever make her careless and willing as Darsh had made Claire in the stories she told about him. It seemed to April that she already knew Darsh, and that he knew her—as if he had sensed her listening to the stories, and was conscious of her interest.

They were almost at the road. April stopped to look back but the hospital buildings were out of sight now, behind the brow of the hill. She turned and walked on. She had one more of these trips to make. The week after that her father would be coming home. He'd been theatrically calm all through their visit, sitting by the window in an easy chair, feet propped on the ottoman, a newspaper across his lap. He was wearing slippers and a cardigan sweater. All he needed was a pipe. He seemed fine, the very picture of health, but that was all it was: a picture. At home he never read the paper. He didn't sit down much, either. The last time April saw him outside the hospital, a month ago, he was under restraint in their landlord's apartment, where he had gone to complain about the shower. He'd been kicking and yelling. His glasses were hanging from one ear. He was shouting at her to call the police, and one of the policemen holding him down was laughing helplessly.

He hadn't crashed yet. He was still flying. April had seen it in his eyes behind the lithium or whatever they were giving him, and she was sure that Claire had seen it too. Claire didn't say anything, but April had been through this with Ellen, her first stepmother, and she'd developed an instinct. She was afraid that Claire had already had enough, that she wasn't going to come back from Italy. Not back to them, anyway. It wouldn't happen according to some plan, it would just happen. April didn't want her to leave, not now. She needed another year. Not even a year—ten months, until she finished school and got herself into college somewhere. If she could cross that line she was sure she could handle whatever came after.

She didn't want Claire to go. Claire had her ways, but she had been good to April, especially in the beginning, when April was always finding fault with her. She'd put up with it. She'd been patient, and let April come to her in her own time. One night April leaned against her when they were reading on the couch, and Claire leaned back, and neither of them drew away. It became their custom to sit like that, braced against each other, reading. Claire thought about things. She had always spoken honestly to April, but with a certain decorum. Now the decorum was gone. Ever since she got the idea that April was "involved" with Stuart, Claire had withdrawn the protections of ceremony and tact, as she would soon withdraw the protections of her income and her care and her presence.

There was no way to change things back. And even if there were, even if by saying "I'm still a virgin" she could turn Claire into some kind of perfect mother, April wouldn't do it. It would sound ridiculous and untrue. And it wasn't true, except as a fact about her body. April did not see virginity as residing in the body. To her it was a quality of the spirit, and something you could only surrender in the spirit. She had done this; she didn't know exactly when or how, but she knew she had done this and she didn't regret it. She did not want to be a virgin and would not pretend to be one, not for anything. When she thought of a virgin she saw someone half-naked, with dumb trusting eyes and flowers woven into her hair, bound at the wrists. She saw a clearing in the jungle, and in the clearing an altar.

Their bus had come and gone, and they had a long wait until the next one. Claire settled on the bench and started reading a book. April had forgotten hers. She sat with Claire for a while, then got up and paced the street when Claire's serenity became intolerable. She walked with her arms crossed and her head bent forward, frowning, scuffing her shoes. Cars rushed past blaring music; a big sailboat on a trailer; a convoy of military trucks, headlights on, soldiers swaying in back. The air was blue with exhaust. April, passing a tire store, looked in the window and saw herself. She squared her shoulders and dropped her arms to her sides, and kept them there by an effort of will as she walked farther up the boulevard to where a line of plastic pennants fluttered over a Toyota lot. A man in a creamy suit was standing in the showroom window, watching the traffic. Even from where she stood April could see the rich drape of his suit. He had high cheekbones, black hair combed straight back from his forehead, a big clean blade of a nose. He looked absolutely self-possessed and possibly dangerous, and April understood that he took some care to be recognized this way. She knew he was aware of her, but he never bothered to turn in her direction. She wandered among the cars, then went back to the bus stop and slumped down on the bench.

"I'm bored," she said.

Claire didn't answer.

"Aren't you bored?"

"Not especially," Claire said. "The bus will be here before long."

"Sure, in about two weeks." April stuck her legs out and knocked the sides of her shoes together. "Let's take a walk," she said.

"I'm all walked out. But you go ahead. Just don't get too far away."

"Not *alone*, Claire. I didn't mean alone. Come on, this is boring." April hated the sound of her voice and she could see that Claire didn't like it either. Claire closed her book. She sat without moving, then said, "I guess I don't have any choice."

April rocked to her feet. She moved a little way off and waited as Claire put the book in her purse, stood, ran her hands down the front of her skirt, and came slowly toward her.

"We'll just stretch our legs," April said. She led Claire up the street to the car lot, where she left the sidewalk and began circling a red Celica convertible.

"I thought you wanted to walk," Claire said.

"Right, just a minute," April said. Then the side door of the showroom swung open and the man in the suit came out. At first he seemed not to know they were there. He knelt beside a sedan and wrote something down on a clipboard. He got up and peered at the sticker on the windshield and wrote something else down. Only then did he permit himself to take notice of them. He looked directly at Claire, and after he'd had a good long look he told her to let him know if she needed anything. His voice had a studied, almost insolent neutrality.

"We're just waiting for a bus," Claire said.

"How does this car stack up against the RX-7?" April asked.

"You surely jest." He made his way toward them through the cars. "I could sell against Mazda any day of the week, if I were selling."

April said, "You're not a salesman?"

He stopped in front of the Celica. "We don't have salesmen here, sugar. We just collect money and try to keep the crowds friendly."

"You've got half of this crowd eating out of your hand," Claire said.

"That's a year old," he said. "Loaded to the gills. Came in last night on a repossession. It'll be gone this time tomorrow. Look at the odometer, sweet pea. What does the odometer say?"

April opened the door and leaned inside. "Four thousand and two," she said. She sat in the driver's seat and worked the gearshift.

"Exactly. Four K. Still on its first tank of gas."

"Little old lady owned it, right?" Claire said.

He gave her another long look before answering. "Little old Marine. Went to the land of the great sand dune and didn't keep up his payments. I've got the keys right here."

"We can't. Sorry, maybe another day."

"I know, you're waiting for a bus. So kill some time."

April got out of the car but left the door open. "Claire, you have to try this seat," she said.

"We should go," Claire said.

"Claire, you just have to. Come on," April said. "Come on, Claire."

The man walked over to the open door and held out his hand. "*Madame*," he said. When Claire stayed where she was, he made a flourish and said, "*Madame! Entrez!*"

Claire walked up to the car. "We really should go," she said. She sat sideways on the seat and swung her legs inside, all in one motion. She nodded at the man and he closed the door. "Yes," he said, "exactly as I thought. The designer was a friend of yours, a very special friend. This automobile was obviously built with you in mind."

"You look great," April said. It was true, and she could see that Claire was in complete possession of that truth. The knowledge was in the set of her mouth, the way her hands came to rest on the wheel.

"There's something missing," the man said. He studied her. "Sunglasses," he said. "A beautiful woman in a convertible has to be wearing sunglasses."

"Put on your sunglasses," April said.

"Please," the man said gently. He leaned against the car and stood over Claire, his back to April, and April understood that she was not to speak again. Her part in this was done; he would close the deal in his own way. He said something in a low voice, and Claire took her sunglasses from her purse and slipped them on. Then she handed him her hat. A gust of heat blew over the lot, rattling the pennants, as April walked toward the showroom. It looked cool in there behind the tinted glass. Quiet. They'd have coffee in the waiting area, old copies of *People*. She could give her feet a rest and catch up on the stars.

The Other Miller

*F*or two days now Miller has been standing in the rain
with the rest of Bravo Company, waiting for some men
from another company to blunder down the logging road
where Bravo waits in ambush. When this happens, if this
happens, Miller will stick his head out of the hole he's hiding in and shoot off all his blank ammunition in the direction of the road. So will everyone else in Bravo Company.
Then they will climb out of their holes and get on some
trucks and go home, back to the base.

This is the plan.

Miller has no faith in it. He has never yet seen a plan
that worked, and this one won't either. His foxhole has
about a foot of water in it. He has to stand on little shelves
he's been digging out of the walls, but the soil is sandy and
the shelves keep collapsing. That means his boots are wet.
Plus his cigarettes are wet. Plus he broke the bridge on his
molars the first night out while chewing up one of the lol-
lipops he'd brought along for energy. It drives him crazy,
the way the broken bridge lifts and grates when he pushes
it with his tongue, but last night he lost his will power and
now he can't keep his tongue away from it.

When he thinks of the other company, the one they're

supposed to ambush, Miller sees a column of dry well-fed men marching farther and farther away from the hole where he stands waiting for them. He sees them moving easily under light packs. He sees them stopping for a smoke break, stretching out on fragrant beds of pine needles under the trees, the murmur of their voices growing more and more faint as one by one they drift into sleep.

It's the truth, by God. Miller knows it like he knows he's going to catch a cold, because that's his luck. If he was in the other company they'd be the ones standing in holes.

Miller's tongue does something to the bridge and a thrill of pain shoots through him. He snaps up straight, eyes burning, teeth clenched against the yell in his throat. He fights it back and glares around him at the other men. The few he can see look stunned and ashen-faced. Of the rest he can make out only their poncho hoods, sticking out of the ground like bullet-shaped rocks.

At this moment, his mind swept clean by pain, Miller can hear the tapping of raindrops on his own poncho. Then he hears the pitchy whine of an engine. A jeep is splashing along the road, slipping from side to side and throwing up thick gouts of mud behind it. The jeep itself is caked with mud. It skids to a stop in front of Bravo Company's position, and the horn beeps twice.

Miller glances around to see what the others are doing. Nobody has moved. They're all just standing in their holes.

The horn beeps again.

A short figure in a poncho emerges from a clump of trees farther up the road. Miller can tell it's the first sergeant by how little he is, so little the poncho hangs almost to his ankles. The first sergeant walks slowly toward the jeep, big blobs of mud all around his boots. When he gets to the jeep he leans his head inside; a moment later he pulls it out. He looks down at the road. He kicks at one of the tires in a thoughtful way. Then he looks up and shouts Miller's name.

Miller keeps watching him. Not until the first sergeant shouts his name again does Miller begin the hard work of hoisting himself out of the foxhole. The other men turn their gray faces up at him as he trudges past their holes.

"Come here, boy," the first sergeant says. He walks a little distance from the jeep and waves Miller over.

Miller follows him. Something is wrong. Miller can tell because the first sergeant called him "boy" instead of "shit-bird." Already he feels a burning in his left side, where his ulcer is.

The first sergeant stares down the road. "Here's the thing," he begins. He stops and turns to Miller. "Goddamn it, anyway. Did you know your mother was sick?"

Miller doesn't say anything, just pushes his lips tight together.

"She must have been sick, right?" Miller remains silent, and the first sergeant says, "She passed away last night. I'm real sorry." He looks sadly up at Miller, and Miller watches his right arm beginning to rise under the poncho; then it falls to his side again. Miller can see that the first sergeant wants to give his shoulder a man-to-man kind of squeeze, but it just wouldn't work. You can only do that if you're taller than the other fellow or at least the same size.

"These boys here will drive you back to base," the first sergeant says, nodding toward the jeep. "You give the Red Cross a call and they'll take it from there. Get yourself some rest," he adds, then walks off toward the trees.

Miller retrieves his gear. One of the men he passes on his way back to the jeep says, "Hey, Miller, what's the story?"

Miller doesn't answer. He's afraid if he opens his mouth he'll start laughing and ruin everything. He keeps his head down and his lips tight as he climbs into the backseat of the jeep, and he doesn't look up until they've left the company a mile or so behind. The fat PFC sitting beside the driver is watching him. He says, "I'm sorry about your mother. That's a bummer."

"Maximum bummer," says the driver, another PFC. He shoots a look over his shoulder. Miller sees his own face reflected for an instant in the driver's sunglasses.

"Had to happen someday," he mumbles, and looks down again.

Miller's hands are shaking. He puts them between his knees and stares through the snapping plastic window at the trees going past. Raindrops rattle on the canvas overhead. He is inside, and everyone else is still outside. Miller can't stop thinking about the others standing around getting rained on, and the thought makes him want to laugh and slap his leg. This is the luckiest he has ever been.

"My grandmother died last year," the driver says. "But that's not the same thing as losing your mother. I feel for you, Miller."

"Don't worry about me," Miller tells him. "I'll get along."

The fat PFC beside the driver says, "Look, don't feel like you have to repress just because we're here. If you want to cry or anything, just go ahead. Right, Leb?"

The driver nods. "Just let it out."

"No problem," Miller says. He wishes he could set these fellows straight so they won't feel like they have to act mournful all the way to Fort Ord. But if he tells them what happened, they'll turn right around and drive him back to his foxhole.

Miller knows what happened. There's another Miller in the battalion with the same initials he's got, W.P., and this Miller is the one whose mother has died. The Army screws up their mail all the time, and now they've screwed this up.

Miller got the whole picture as soon as the first sergeant started asking about his mother.

For once, everybody else is on the outside and Miller is on the inside. Inside, on his way to a hot shower, dry clothes, a pizza, and a warm bunk. He didn't even have to do anything wrong to get here; he just did as he was told. It was their own mistake. Tomorrow he'll rest up like the first sergeant ordered him to, go on sick call about his bridge, maybe downtown to a movie after that. Then he'll call the Red Cross. By the time they get everything straightened out it will be too late to send him back to the field. And the best thing is, the other Miller won't know. The other Miller will have a whole other day of thinking his mother is still alive. You could even say that Miller is keeping her alive for him.

The man beside the driver turns around again and studies Miller. He has small dark eyes in a big white face covered with beads of sweat. His name tag reads KAISER. Showing little square teeth like a baby's, he says, "You're really coping, Miller. Most guys pretty much lose it when they get the word."

"I would too," the driver says. "Anybody would. It's *human*, Kaiser."

"For sure," Kaiser says. "I'm not saying I'm any different. That's going to be my worst day, the day my mom dies." He blinks rapidly, but not before Miller sees his little eyes mist up.

"Everybody has to go sometime," Miller says, "sooner or later. That's my philosophy."

"Heavy," the driver says. "Really deep."

Kaiser gives him a sharp look and says, "At ease, Lebowitz."

Miller leans forward. Lebowitz is a Jewish name. That means Lebowitz must be a Jew. Miller wants to ask him why he's in the Army, but he's afraid Lebowitz might take it wrong. Instead he says conversationally, "You don't see too many Jewish people in the Army nowadays."

Lebowitz looks into the rearview. His thick eyebrows arch over his sunglasses, then he shakes his head and says something Miller can't make out.

"At ease, Leb," Kaiser says again. He turns to Miller and asks him where the funeral is going to be held.

"What funeral?" Miller says.

Lebowitz laughs.

"Fuckhead," Kaiser says. "Haven't you ever heard of shock?"

Lebowitz is quiet for a moment. Then he looks into the rearview again and says, "Sorry, Miller. I was out of line."

Miller shrugs. His probing tongue pushes the bridge too hard and he stiffens suddenly.

"Where did your mom live?" Kaiser asks.

"Redding," Miller says.

Kaiser nods. "Redding," he repeats. He keeps watching Miller. So does Lebowitz, glancing back and forth between the mirror and the road. Miller understands that they expected a different kind of performance than the one he's giving them, more emotional and all. They've seen other personnel whose mothers died and now they have certain standards he has failed to live up to. He looks out the window. They're driving along a ridgeline. Slices of blue flicker between the trees on the left-hand side of the road; then they hit a space without trees and Miller can see the ocean below them, clear to the horizon under a bright cloudless sky. Except for a few hazy wisps in the treetops they've left the clouds behind, back in the mountains, hanging over the soldiers there.

"Don't get me wrong," Miller says. "I'm sorry she's dead."

Kaiser says, "That's the way. Talk it out."

"It's just that I didn't know her all that well," Miller

says, and after this monstrous lie a feeling of weightlessness comes over him. At first it makes him uncomfortable, but almost immediately he begins to enjoy it. From now on he can say anything.

He makes a sad face. "I guess I'd be more broken up and so on if she hadn't taken off on us the way she did. Right in the middle of harvest season. Just leaving us flat like that."

"I'm hearing a lot of anger," Kaiser tells him. "Ventilate. Own it."

Miller got that stuff from a song, but he can't remember any more. He lowers his head and looks at his boots. "Killed my dad," he says after a time. "Died of a broken heart. Left me with five kids to raise, not to mention the farm." Miller closes his eyes. He sees a field all ploughed up and the sun setting behind it, a bunch of kids coming in from the field with rakes and hoes on their shoulders. While the jeep winds down through the switchbacks he describes his hardships as the oldest child in this family. He is at the end of his story when they reach the coast highway and turn north. All at once the jeep stops rattling and swaying. They pick up speed. The tires hum on the smooth road. The rushing air whistles a single note around the radio antenna. "Anyway," Miller says, "it's been two years since I even had a letter from her."

"You should make a movie," Lebowitz says.

Miller isn't sure how to take this. He waits to hear what else Lebowitz has to say, but Lebowitz is silent. So is Kaiser, who's had his back turned to Miller for several minutes now. Both men stare at the road ahead of them. Miller can see that they've lost interest. He feels disappointed, because he was having a fine time pulling their leg.

One thing Miller told them was true: he hasn't had a letter from his mother in two years. She wrote him a lot when he first joined the Army, at least once a week, sometimes twice, but Miller sent all her letters back unopened and after a year of this she finally gave up. She tried calling a few times but Miller wouldn't go to the telephone, so she gave that up too. Miller wants her to understand that her son is not a man to turn the other cheek. He is a serious man. Once you've crossed him, you've lost him.

Miller's mother crossed him by marrying a man she shouldn't have married. Phil Dove. Dove was a biology teacher in the high school. Miller was having trouble in the course, so his mother went to talk to Dove about it and ended up getting engaged to him. When Miller tried to reason with her, she wouldn't hear a word. You would think from the way she acted that she'd landed herself a real catch instead of someone who talked with a stammer and spent his life taking crayfish apart.

Miller did everything he could to stop the marriage, but his mother had blinded herself. She couldn't see what she already had, how good it was with just the two of them. How he was always there when she got home from work, with a pot of coffee all brewed up. The two of them drinking their coffee together and talking about different things, or maybe not talking at all—maybe just sitting in the kitchen while the room got dark around them, until the telephone rang or the dog started whining to get out. Walking the dog around the reservoir. Coming back and eating whatever they wanted to eat, sometimes nothing, sometimes the same dish three or four nights in a row, watching the programs they wanted to watch and going to bed when they wanted to and not because some other person wanted them to. Just being together in their own place.

Phil Dove got Miller's mother so mixed up she forgot how good their life was. She refused to see what she was ruining. "You'll be leaving anyway," she told him. "You'll be moving on, next year or the year after"—which showed how wrong she was about Miller, because he would never have left her, not ever, not for anything. But when he said this she laughed as if she knew better, as if he wasn't serious. He was serious, though. He was serious when he promised he'd stay, and he was serious when he promised he'd never speak to her again if she married Phil Dove.

She married him. Miller stayed at a motel that night and two nights more, until he ran out of money. Then he joined the Army. He knew that would get to her, because he was still a month shy of finishing high school, and because his father had been killed while serving in the Army. Not in Vietnam but in Georgia, in an accident. He and another man were dipping mess kits in a garbage can full of boiling water and somehow the can fell over on him. Miller was six at the time. Miller's mother hated the Army after that, not because her husband was dead—she knew about the war he was going to, she knew about ambushes and mines—but because of the way it happened. She said the Army couldn't even get a man killed in a decent fashion.

She was right, too. The Army was just as bad as she thought, and worse. You spent all your time waiting around. You lived a completely stupid existence. Miller hated every minute of it, but there was pleasure in his hatred because he believed that his mother must know how unhappy he was. That knowledge would be a grief to her. It would not be as bad as the grief she had given him, which was spreading from his heart into his stomach and teeth and everywhere else, but it was the worst grief he had power to cause, and it would serve to keep her in mind of him.

Kaiser and Lebowitz are describing hamburgers to each other. Their idea of the perfect hamburger. Miller tries not to listen but their voices go on, and after a while he can't think of anything but beefsteak tomatoes and Gulden's mustard and steaming, onion-stuffed meat crisscrossed with black marks from the grill. He is at the point of asking them to change the subject when Kaiser turns and says, "Think you can handle some chow?"

"I don't know," Miller says. "I guess I could get something down."

"We were talking about a pit stop. But if you want to keep going, just say the word. It's your ball game. I mean, technically we're supposed to take you straight back to base."

"I could eat," Miller says.

"That's the spirit. At a time like this you've got to keep your strength up."

"I could eat," Miller says again.

Lebowitz looks up into the rearview mirror, shakes his head, and looks away again.

They take the next turn-off and drive inland to a crossroads where two gas stations face two restaurants. One of the restaurants is boarded up, so Lebowitz pulls into the parking lot of the Dairy Queen across the road. He turns the engine off, and the three men sit motionless in the sudden silence. Then Miller hears the distant clang of metal on metal, the caw of a crow, the creak of Kaiser shifting in his seat. A dog barks in front of a rust-streaked trailer next door. A skinny white dog with yellow eyes. As it barks the dog rubs itself, one leg raised and twitching, against a sign that shows an outspread hand below the words "KNOW YOUR FUTURE."

They get out of the jeep and Miller follows Kaiser and Lebowitz across the parking lot. The air is warm and smells of oil. In the gas station across the road a pink-skinned man in a swimming suit is trying to put air in the tires of his bicycle, jerking at the hose and swearing loudly. Miller pushes his tongue against the broken bridge, lifting it gently. He wonders if he should try eating a hamburger, and decides it can't hurt as long as he's careful to chew on the other side of his mouth.

But it does hurt. After the first couple of bites Miller shoves his plate away. He rests his chin on one hand and listens to Lebowitz and Kaiser argue about whether people can actually tell the future. Lebowitz is talking about a girl he used to know who had ESP. "We'd be driving along," he says, "and out of the blue she would tell me exactly what I was thinking about. It was unbelievable."

Kaiser finishes his hamburger and takes a drink of milk. "No big deal," he says. "I could do that." He pulls Miller's hamburger over to his side of the table and takes a bite out of it.

"Go ahead," Lebowitz says. "Try it. I'm not thinking about what you think I'm thinking about."

"Yes you are."

"All right, now I am," Lebowitz says, "but I wasn't before."

"I wouldn't let a fortune-teller get near me," Miller says. "The way I see it, the less you know the better off you are."

"More vintage philosophy from the private stock of W. P. Miller," Lebowitz says. He looks at Kaiser, who is eating the last of Miller's hamburger. "Well, how about it? I'm up for it if you are."

Kaiser chews ruminatively. He swallows and licks his lips. "Sure," he says. "Why not? As long as Miller here doesn't mind."

"Mind what?" Miller asks.

Lebowitz stands and puts his sunglasses back on. "Don't worry about Miller. Miller's cool. Miller keeps his head when men all around him are losing theirs."

Kaiser and Miller get up from the table and follow Lebowitz outside. Lebowitz is bending down in the shade of a dumpster, wiping off his boots with a handkerchief.

Shiny blue flies buzz around him. "Mind what?" Miller repeats.

"We thought we'd check out the prophet," Kaiser tells him.

Lebowitz straightens up and the three of them start across the parking lot.

"I'd actually kind of like to get going," Miller says. When they reach the jeep he stops, but Lebowitz and Kaiser walk on. "Now listen," Miller says, and skips a little to catch up. "I have a lot to do," he says to their backs. "I have to get home."

"We know how broken up you are," Lebowitz tells him. He keeps walking.

"This won't take too long," Kaiser says.

The dog barks once and then, when it sees that they really intend to come within range of his teeth, runs around the trailer. Lebowitz knocks on the door. It swings open, and there stands a round-faced woman with dark, sunken eyes and heavy lips. One of her eyes has a cast; it seems to be watching something beside her while the other looks down at the three soldiers at her door. Her hands are covered with flour. She is a gypsy, an actual gypsy. Miller has never seen a gypsy before, but he recognizes her as surely as he would recognize a wolf if he saw one. Her presence makes his blood pound in his veins. If he lived in this place he would come back at night with other men, all of them yelling and waving torches, and drive her out.

"You on duty?" Lebowitz asks.

She nods, wiping her hands on her skirt. They leave chalky streaks on the bright patchwork. "All of you?" she asks.

"You bet," Kaiser says. His voice is unnaturally loud.

She nods again and turns her good eye from Lebowitz to Kaiser, then to Miller. Gazing at Miller, she smiles and rattles off a string of strange sounds, words from another language or maybe a spell, as if she expects him to understand. One of her front teeth is black.

"No," Miller says. "No, ma'am. Not me." He shakes his head.

"Come," she says, and stands aside.

Lebowitz and Kaiser mount the steps and disappear into the trailer. "Come," the woman repeats. She beckons with her white hands.

Miller backs away, still shaking his head. "Leave me alone," he tells her, and before she can answer he turns and walks away. He goes back to the jeep and sits in the driver's seat, leaving both doors open to catch the breeze. Miller feels the heat drawing the dampness out of his fatigues. He can smell the musty wet canvas overhead and the sourness of his own body. Through the windshield, covered with mud except for a pair of grimy half-circles, he watches three boys solemnly urinating against the wall of the gas station across the road.

Miller bends down to loosen his boots. Blood rushes to his face as he fights the wet laces, and his breath comes faster and faster. "Goddamn laces," he says. "Goddamn rain." He gets the laces untied and sits up, panting. He stares at the trailer. Goddamn gypsy.

He can't believe those two fools actually went inside there. Yukking it up. Playing around. That shows how stupid they are, because anybody knows that you don't play around with fortune-tellers. There's no predicting what a fortune-teller might say, and once it's said, no way of keeping it from happening. Once you hear what's out there it isn't out there anymore, it's here. You might as well open your door to a murderer as to the future.

The future. Didn't everybody know enough about the future already, without rooting around for the details? There is only one thing you have to know about the future:

everything gets worse. Once you have that, you have it all. The specifics don't bear thinking about.

Miller certainly has no intention of thinking about the specifics. He peels off his damp socks and massages his crinkled white feet. Now and then he glances up toward the trailer, where the gypsy is pronouncing fate on Kaiser and Lebowitz. Miller makes humming noises. He will not think about the future.

Because it's true—everything gets worse. One day you're sitting in front of your house poking sticks into an anthill, hearing the chink of silverware and the voices of your mother and father in the kitchen; then, at some moment you can't even remember, one of those voices is gone. And you never hear it again. When you go from today to tomorrow you're walking into an ambush.

What lies ahead doesn't bear thinking about. Already Miller has an ulcer, and his teeth are full of holes. His body is giving out on him. What will it be like when he's sixty? Or even five years from now? Miller was in a restaurant the other day and saw a fellow about his own age in a wheelchair, getting fed soup by a woman who was talking to some other people at the table. This boy's hands lay twisted in his lap like gloves somebody dropped there. His pants had crawled up halfway to his knees, showing pale wasted legs no thicker than bones. He could barely move his head. The woman feeding him did a lousy job because she was too busy blabbing to her friends. Half the soup went onto the boy's shirt. Yet his eyes were bright and attentive. Miller thought: That could happen to me.

You could be going along just fine and then one day, through no fault of your own, something could get loose in your bloodstream and knock out part of your brain. Leave you like that. And if it didn't happen now, all at once, it was sure to happen slowly later on. That was the end you were bound for.

Someday Miller is going to die. He knows that, and he prides himself on knowing it when everyone else only pretends to, secretly believing that they will live forever. But this is not the reason the future is unthinkable to him. There is something else worse than that, something not to be considered, and he will not consider it.

He will not consider it. Miller leans back against the seat and closes his eyes, but his effort to trick himself into somnolence fails; behind his eyelids he is wide awake and fidgety with gloom, probing against his will for what he is afraid to find, until, with no surprise at all, he finds it. A simple truth. His mother is also going to die. Just like him. And there is no telling when. Miller cannot count on her to be there to come home to, and receive his pardon, when he finally decides that she has suffered enough.

Miller opens his eyes and looks at the raw shapes of the buildings across the road, their outlines lost through the grime on the windshield. He closes his eyes again. He listens to himself breathe and feels the familiar, almost muscular ache of knowing that he is beyond his mother's reach. That he has put himself where she cannot see him or speak to him or touch him in that thoughtless way of hers, resting her hands on his shoulders as she stops behind his chair to ask him a question or just rest for a moment, her mind somewhere else. This was supposed to be her punishment, but somehow it has become his own. He understands that it has to stop. It is killing him.

It has to stop now, and as if he has been planning for this day all along Miller knows exactly what he will do. Instead of reporting to the Red Cross when he gets back to base, he will pack his bag and catch the first bus home. No one will blame him for this. Even when they discover the mistake they've made they still won't blame him, because it would be the natural thing for a grieving son to do. Instead of punishing him they will probably apologize for giving him a scare.

He will take the first bus home, express or not. It will be full of Mexicans and soldiers. Miller will sit by a window and drowse. Now and then he will come up from his dreams to stare out at the passing green hills and loamy ploughland and the stations where the bus puts in, stations cloudy with exhaust and loud with engine roar, where the people he regards through his window will look groggily back at him as if they too have just come up from sleep. Salinas. Vacaville. Red Bluff. When he gets to Redding Miller will hire a cab. He will ask the driver to stop at Schwartz's for a few minutes while he buys some flowers, and then he will ride on home, down Sutter and over to Serra, past the ball park, past the grade school, past the Mormon church. Right on Belmont. Left on Park. Leaning over the seat, saying Farther, farther, a little farther, that's it, that one, there.

The sound of voices behind the door as he rings the bell. Door swings open, voices hush. Who are these people? Men in suits, women wearing white gloves. Someone stammers his name, strange to him now, almost forgotten. W-W-Wesley. A man's voice. Miller stands just inside the door, breathing perfume. Then the flowers are taken from his hand and laid with other flowers on the coffee table. He hears his name again. It is Phil Dove, moving toward him from across the room. He walks slowly, with his arms raised, like a blind man.

Wesley, he says. Thank God you're home.

Two Boys and a Girl

Gilbert saw her first. This was in late June, at a party. She was sitting alone in the backyard, stretched out on a lawn chair, when he went to get a beer from the cooler. He tried to think of something to say to her, but she seemed complete in her solitude and he was afraid of sounding intrusive and obvious. Later he saw her again, inside—a pale, dark-haired girl with dark eyes and lipstick smears on her teeth. She was dancing with Gilbert's best friend, Rafe. The night after that she was with Rafe when he picked Gilbert up to go to another party, and again the night after that. Her name was Mary Ann.

Mary Ann, Rafe, and Gilbert. They went everywhere together that summer, to parties and movies and the lake, to the pools of friends, and on long aimless drives after Gilbert got off work at his father's bookstore. Gilbert didn't have a car, so Rafe did the driving; his grandfather had given him his immaculate old Buick convertible as a reward for getting into Yale. Mary Ann leaned against him with her bare white feet up on the dash, while Gilbert sprawled like a pasha in the back and handed out the beers and made ironic comment on whatever attracted his notice.

Gilbert was deeply ironic. At the high school where he and Rafe had been classmates, the yearbook editors voted him Most Cynical. That pleased him. Gilbert believed disillusionment to be the natural consequence, even the duty, of a mind that could cut through the authorized version to the true nature of things. He made it his business to take nothing on trust, to respect no authority but that of his own judgment, and to be elegantly unsurprised at the grossest crimes and follies, especially those of the world's anointed.

Mary Ann listened to what he said, even when she seemed to be occupied with Rafe. Gilbert knew this, and he knew when he'd managed to shock her. She clenched her hands, blinked rapidly, and a red splotch, vivid as a birthmark, appeared on the milky skin of her neck. It wasn't hard to shock Mary Ann. Her father, a captain in the Coast Guard, was the squarest human being Gilbert had ever met. One night when he and Rafe were waiting for Mary Ann, Captain McCoy stared at Gilbert's sandals and asked what he thought about the beatniks. Mrs. McCoy had doilies all over the house, and pictures of kittens and the Holy Land and dogs playing poker, and in the toilets these chemical gizmos that turned the water blue. Gilbert felt sorry for Mary Ann whenever he took a leak at her house.

In early August, Rafe went fishing in Canada with his father. He left Gilbert the keys to the Buick and told him to take care of Mary Ann. Gilbert recognized this as what the hero of a war movie says to his drab sidekick before leaving on the big mission.

Rafe delivered his instructions while he was in his room packing for the trip. Gilbert lounged on the bed watching him. He wanted to talk but Rafe was playing his six-record set of *I Pagliacci*, which Gilbert didn't believe he really liked, though Rafe made occasional humming noises as if he knew the whole score by heart. Gilbert thought he was taking up opera the same way he'd taken up squash that winter, as an accessory. He lay back and was silent. Rafe went about his business; he was graceful and precise, and he assembled his gear without waste of motion or hesitation as to where things were. At one point he walked over to the mirror and studied himself as if he were alone, and Gilbert was surprised by the anger he felt. Then Rafe turned to him and tossed the keys on the bed and spoke his line about taking care of Mary Ann.

The next day Gilbert drove the Buick around town all by himself. He double-parked in front of Nordstrom's with the top down and smoked cigarettes and watched the women come out as if he were waiting for one of them. Now and then he examined his watch and frowned. He drove onto a pier at the wharf and waved at one of the passengers on the boat to Victoria. She was looking down at the water and didn't see him until she raised her eyes as the boat was backing out of the slip, and caught him blowing her a kiss. She stepped away from the rail and vanished from sight. Later he went to La Luna, a bar near the university where he knew he wouldn't get carded, and took a seat from which he could see the Buick. When the bar filled up he walked outside and raised the hood and checked the oil, right in front of La Luna's big picture window. To a couple walking past he said, "This damn thing drinks oil like it's going out of style." Then he drove off with the expression of a man with important and not entirely pleasant business to perform. He stopped and bought cigarettes in two different drugstores. He called home from the second drugstore and told his mother he wouldn't be in for dinner and asked if he'd gotten any mail. No, his mother said, nothing. Gilbert ate at a drive-in and cruised for a while and then went up to the lookout above Alki Point and sat on the hood of the Buick and smoked in a moody, philosophical way, deliberately ignoring the girls with their dates in the cars around him. A heavy mist stole in from the sound. Across the water the lights of the city blurred, and a foghorn began to call. Gilbert flipped his cigarette into the shadows and rubbed his bare arms. When he got home he called Mary Ann, and they agreed to go to a movie the following night.

After the movie Gilbert drove Mary Ann back to her house, but instead of getting out of the car she sat where she was and they went on talking. It was easy, easier than he'd imagined. When Rafe was with them, Gilbert could speak through him to Mary Ann and be witty or deep or outrageous. In the moments they'd been alone, waiting for Rafe to rejoin them, he had always found himself tongue-tied, in a kind of panic. He'd cudgel his brains for something to say, and whatever he did come up with sounded tense and sharp. But that didn't happen, not that night.

It was raining hard. When Gilbert saw that Mary Ann wasn't in any hurry to get out, he cut the engine and they sat there in the faint marine light of the radio tuning band with liquid shadows playing over their faces from the rain streaming down the windows. The rain drummed in gusts on the canvas roof but inside it was warm and close, like a tent during a storm. Mary Ann was talking about nursing school, about her fear that she wouldn't measure up in the tough courses, especially Anatomy and Physiology. Gilbert thought she was being ritually humble and said, Oh, come on, you'll do fine.

I don't know, she said. I just don't know. And then she told him how badly she'd done in science and math, and how two of her teachers had personally gone down to the nursing-school admissions office to help her get in. Gilbert saw that she really was afraid of failing, and that she had reason to be afraid. Now that she'd said so herself, it made sense to him that she struggled in school. She wasn't quick that way; wasn't clever. There was a simplicity about her.

She leaned back into the corner, watching the rain. She looked sad. Gilbert thought of touching her cheek with the back of his hand to reassure her. He waited a moment, then told her it wasn't exactly true that he was trying to make up his mind whether to go to the University of Washington or Amherst. He should have corrected that misunderstanding before. The actual truth was, he hadn't gotten into Amherst. He'd made it onto the waiting list, but with only three weeks left until school began he figured his odds were just about nil.

She turned and regarded him. He couldn't see her eyes. They were dark pools with only a glint of light at the bottom. She asked why he hadn't gotten in.

To this question Gilbert had no end of answers. He thought of new ones every day, and was sick of them all. I stopped working, he said. I just completely slacked off.

But you should've gotten in wherever you wanted. You're smart enough.

I talk a pretty good game, I guess. He took out a cigarette and tapped the end against the steering wheel. I don't know why I smoke these damn things, he said.

You like the way they make you look. Intellectual.

I guess. He lit it.

She watched him closely as he took the first drag. Let me, she said. Just a puff.

Their fingers touched when he handed her the cigarette.

You're going to be a great nurse, he said.

She took a puff of the cigarette and blew the smoke out slowly.

Neither of them spoke for a time.

I'd better go in, she said.

Gilbert watched her go up the walkway to her house. She didn't hunch and run but moved sedately through the lashing rain, as if this were a night like any other. He waited until he saw her step inside, then turned the radio back up and drove away. He kept tasting her lipstick on the cigarette.

When he called from work the next day her mother answered and asked him to wait. Mary Ann was out of breath when she came to the phone. She said she'd been outside on a ladder, helping her dad paint the house. What are you up to? she asked.

I was just wondering what you were doing, he said.

He took her to La Luna that night, and the next. Both times they got the same booth, right near the jukebox. "Don't Think Twice, It's All Right" had just come out and Mary Ann played it again and again while they talked. On the third night some guys in baseball uniforms were sitting there when they came in. Gilbert was annoyed and saw that she was too. They sat at the bar for a time but kept getting jostled by the drinkers behind them. They decided to go someplace else. Gilbert was paying his tab when the baseball players stood up to leave, and Mary Ann slipped into the booth just ahead of an older couple who'd been waiting nearby.

We were here first, the woman said to Mary Ann as Gilbert sat down across from her.

This is our booth, Mary Ann said, in a friendly, informative way.

How do you figure that?

Mary Ann looked at the woman as if she'd asked a truly eccentric question. Well, I don't know, she said. It just is.

Afterward it kept coming back to Gilbert, the way Mary Ann had said "our booth." He collected such observations and pondered them when he was away from her: her breathlessness when she came to the phone, the habit she'd formed of taking puffs from his cigarettes and helping herself to his change to play the jukebox, the way she listened to him with such open credulity that he found it impossible to brag or make excuses or say things merely for effect. He couldn't be facetious with Mary Ann. She always thought he meant exactly what he said, and then he had to stop and try to explain that he'd actually meant something else. His irony began to sound weak and somehow envious. It sounded thin and unmanly.

Mary Ann gave him no occasion for it. She took him seriously. She wrote down the names of the books he spoke of—*On the Road*, *The Stranger*, *The Fountainhead*, and some others that he hadn't actually read but knew about and intended to read as soon as he found the time. She listened when he explained what was wrong with Barry Goldwater and *Reader's Digest* and the television shows she liked, and agreed that he was probably right. In the solemnity of her attention he heard himself saying things he had said to no one else, confessing hopes so implausible he had barely confessed them to himself. He was often surprised by his own honesty. But he stopped short of telling Mary Ann what was most on his mind, and what he believed she already knew, because of the chance that she didn't know or wasn't ready to admit she did. Once he said it, everything would change, for all of them, and he wasn't prepared to risk this.

They went out every night but two, once when Gilbert had to work overtime and once when Captain McCoy took Mary Ann and her mother to dinner. They saw a couple more movies and went to a party and to La Luna and drove around the city. The nights were warm and clear and Gilbert put the top down and poked along in the right lane. He used to wonder, with some impatience, why Rafe drove so slowly. Now he knew. To command the wheel of an open car with a girl on the seat beside you was to be established in a condition that only a fool would hasten to end. He drove slowly around the lake and downtown and up to the lookouts and then back to Mary Ann's house. The first few nights they sat in the car. After that, Mary Ann invited Gilbert inside.

He talked; she talked. She talked about her little sister, Colleen, who had died of cystic fibrosis two years before, and whose long hard dying had brought her family close and given her the idea of becoming a nurse. She talked about friends from school and the nuns who had taught her. She talked about her parents and grandparents and Rafe. All her talk was of her affections. Unconditional enthusiasm generally had a wearying effect on Gilbert, but Mary Ann gave praise, it seemed to him, not to shine it back on herself or to dissemble some secret bitterness but because that was her nature. That was how she was, and he liked her for it, as he liked it that she didn't question everything but trusted freely, like a child.

She had been teaching herself the guitar, and sometimes she would consent to play and sing for him, old ballads about mine disasters and nice lads getting hanged for poaching and noblewomen drowning their babies. He could see how the words moved her: so much that her voice would give out for moments at a time, during which she would bite her lower lip and gaze down at the floor. She put folk songs on the record player and listened to them with her eyes closed. She also liked Roy Orbison and the Fleetwoods and Ray Charles. One night she was bringing some fudge from the kitchen just as "Born to Lose" came on. Gilbert stood and offered his hand with a dandified flourish that she could have laughed off if she'd chosen to. She put the plate down and took his hand and they began to dance, stiffly at first, from a distance, then easily and close. They fit perfectly. Perfectly. He felt the rub of her hips and thighs, the heat of her skin. Her warm hand tightened in his. He breathed in the scent of lavender water with the sunny smell of her hair and the faint salt smell of her body. He breathed it all in again and again. And then he felt himself grow hard and rise against her, so that she had to know, she just had to know, and he waited for her to move away. But she did not move away. She pressed close to him until the song ended, and for a moment or two after. Then she stepped back and let go of Gilbert's hand and in a hoarse voice asked him if he wanted some fudge. She was facing him but managing not to look at him.

Maybe later, he said, and held out his hand again. May I have the honor?

She walked over to the couch and sat down. I'm so clumsy.

No you're not. You're a great dancer.

She shook her head.

He sat down in the chair across from her. She still wouldn't look at him. She put her hands together and stared at them.

Then she said, How come Rafe's dad picks on him all the time?

I don't know. There isn't any particular reason. Bad chemistry, I guess.

It's like he can't do anything right. His dad won't let him alone, even when I'm there. I bet he's having a miserable time.

It was true that neither Rafe's father nor his mother took much pleasure in their son. Gilbert had no idea why this should be so. But it was a strange subject to have boiled up out of nowhere like this, and for her to be suddenly close to tears about. Don't worry about Rafe, he said. Rafe can take care of himself.

The grandfather clock chimed the Westminster Bells, then struck twelve times. The clock had been made to go with the living room ensemble and its tone, tinny and untrue, set Gilbert on edge. The whole house set him on edge: the pictures, the matching Colonial furniture, the single bookshelf full of condensed books. It was like a house Russian spies would practice being Americans in.

It's just so unfair, Mary Ann said. Rafe is so sweet.

He's a good egg, Rafe, Gilbert said. Most assuredly. One of the best.

He is the best.

Gilbert got up to leave and Mary Ann did look at him then, with something like alarm. She stood and followed him outside onto the porch. When he looked back from the end of the walkway, she was watching him with her arms crossed over her chest. Call me tomorrow, she said. Okay?

I was thinking of doing some reading, he said. Then he said, I'll see. I'll see how things go.

The next night they went bowling. This was Mary Ann's idea. She was a good bowler and frankly out to win. Whenever she got a strike she threw her head back and gave a great bark of triumph. She questioned Gilbert's scorekeeping until he got rattled and told her to take over, which she did without even a show of protest. When she guttered her ball she claimed she'd slipped on a wet spot and insisted on bowling that frame again. He didn't let her, he understood that she would despise him if he did, but her shamelessness somehow made him happier than he'd been all day.

As he pulled up to her house Mary Ann said, Next time I'll give you some pointers. You'd be half decent if you knew what you were doing.

Hearing that "next time," he killed the engine and turned and looked at her. Mary Ann, he said.

He had never said so much before.

She looked straight ahead and didn't answer. Then she said, I'm thirsty. You want a glass of juice or something? Before Gilbert could say anything, she added, We'll have to sit outside, okay? I think we woke my dad up last night.

Gilbert waited on the steps while Mary Ann went into the house. Paint cans and brushes were arranged on top of the porch railing. Captain McCoy scraped and painted one side of the house every year. This year he was doing the front. That was just like him, to eke it out one side at a time. Gilbert had once helped the Captain make crushed ice for drinks. The way the Captain did it, he held a single cube in his hand and clobbered it with a hammer until it was pulverized. Then another cube. Then another. Etcetera. When Gilbert wrapped a whole tray's worth in a hand towel and started to whack it against the counter, the Captain grabbed the towel away from him. That's not how you do it! he said. He found Gilbert another hammer and the two of them stood there hitting cube after cube.

Mary Ann came out with two glasses of orange juice. She sat beside Gilbert and they drank and looked out at the Buick gleaming under the streetlight.

I'm off tomorrow, Gilbert said. You want to go for a drive?

Gee, I wish I could. I promised my dad I'd paint the fence.

We'll paint, then.

That's all right. It's your day off. You should do something.

Painting's something.

Something you like, dummy.

I like to paint. In fact I love painting.

Gilbert.

No kidding, I love to paint. Ask my folks. Every free minute, I'm out there with a brush.

Like fun.

So what time do we start? Look, it's only been three hours since I did my last fence and already my hand's starting to shake.

Stop it! I don't know. Whenever. After breakfast.

He finished his juice and rolled the glass between his hands. Mary Ann.

He felt her hesitate. Yes?

He kept rolling the glass. What do your folks think about us going out so much?

They don't mind. I think they're glad, actually.

I'm not exactly their type.

Hah. You can say that again.

What're they so glad about then?

You're not Rafe.

What, they don't like Rafe?

Oh, they like him, a lot. A whole lot. They're always saying how if they had a son, and so on. But my dad thinks we're getting too serious.

Ah, too serious. So I'm comic relief.

Don't say that.

I'm not comic relief?

No.

Gilbert put his elbows on the step behind him. He looked up at the sky and said carefully, He'll be back in a couple of days.

I know.

Then what?

She leaned forward and stared into the yard as if she'd heard a sound.

He waited for a time, aware of every breath he took. Then what? he said again.

I don't know. Maybe . . . I don't know. I'm really kind of tired. You're coming tomorrow, right?

If that's what you want.

You said you were.

Only if you want me to.

I want you to.

Okay. Sure. Tomorrow, then.

Gilbert stopped at a diner on the way home. He ate a piece of apple pie, then drank coffee and watched the cars go past. To an ordinary person driving by he supposed he must look pretty tragic, sitting here alone over a coffee cup, cigarette smoke curling past his face. And the strange thing was, that person would be right. He was about to betray his best friend. To cut Rafe off from the two people he trusted most, possibly, he understood, from trust itself. Himself, too, he would betray—his belief, held deep under the stream of his flippancy, that he was steadfast and loyal. And he knew what he was doing. That was why this whole thing was tragic, because he knew what he was doing and could not do otherwise.

He had thought it all out. He could provide himself with reasons. Rafe and Mary Ann would have broken up anyway, sooner or later. Rafe was moving on. He didn't know it, but he was leaving them behind. He'd have room-mates, guys from rich families who'd invite him home for vacation, take him skiing, sailing. He'd wear a tuxedo to debutante parties where he'd meet girls from Smith and Mount Holyoke, philosophy majors, English majors, girls with ideas who were reading the same books he was reading and other books too, who could say things he wouldn't have expected them to say. He'd get interested in one of these girls and go on road trips with his friends to her college. She'd come to New Haven. They'd rendezvous in Boston and New York. He'd meet her parents. And on the first day of his next trip home, honorable Rafe would enter Mary Ann's house and leave half an hour later with a sorrowful face and a heart leaping with joy. There wouldn't be many more trips home, not after that. What was here to bring him all that way? Not his parents, those crocodiles. Not Mary Ann. Himself? Good old Gilbert? Please.

And Mary Ann, what about Mary Ann? Once Rafe double-timed her and then dropped her cold, what would happen to that simple good-heartedness of hers? Would she begin to suspect it, stand guard over it? He was right to do anything to keep that from happening.

These were the reasons, and they were good reasons, but Gilbert could make no use of them. He knew that he would do what he was going to do even if Rafe stayed at home and went to college with him, or if Mary Ann was somewhat more calculating. Reasons always came with a purpose, to give the appearance of a struggle between principle and desire. But there'd been no struggle. Principle had power only until you found what you had to have.

Captain McCoy was helping Mrs. McCoy into the car when Gilbert pulled up behind him. The Captain waited as his wife gathered her dress inside, then closed the door and walked back toward the Buick. Gilbert came around to meet him.

Mary Ann tells me you're going to help with the fence.

Yes, sir.

There's not that much of it—shouldn't take too long.

They both looked at the fence, about sixty feet of white pickets that ran along the sidewalk. Mary Ann came out on the porch and mimed "hi."

Captain McCoy said, Would you mind picking up the paint? It's that Glidden store down on California. Just give 'em my name. He opened his car door, then looked at the fence again. Scrape her good. That's the secret. Give her a good scraping and the rest'll go easy. And try not to get any paint on the grass.

Mary Ann came through the gate and waved as her parents drove off. She said that they were going over to Bremerton to see her grandmother. Well, she said. You want some coffee or something?

I'm fine.

He followed her up the walk. She had on cutoffs. Her legs were very white and they flexed in a certain way as she climbed the porch steps. Captain McCoy had set out two scrapers and two brushes on the railing, all four of them exactly parallel. Mary Ann handed Gilbert a scraper and they went back to the fence. What a day! she said. Isn't it the most beautiful day? She knelt to the right of the gate and began to scrape. Then she looked back at Gilbert watching her and said, Why don't you do that side over there? We'll see who gets done first.

There wasn't much to scrape, some blisters, a few peeling patches here and there. This fence is in good shape, Gilbert said. How come you're painting it?

It goes with the front. When we paint the front, we always paint the fence.

It doesn't need it. All it needs is some retouching.

I guess. Dad wanted us to paint it, though. He always paints it when he paints the front.

Gilbert looked at the gleaming white house, the bright weedless lawn trimmed to the nap of a crewcut.

Guess who called this morning, Mary Ann said.

Who?

Rafe! There was a big storm coming in so they left early. He'll be back tonight. He sounded really great. He said to say hi.

Gilbert ran the scraper up and down a picket.

It was so good to hear his voice, Mary Ann said. I wish you'd been here to talk to him.

A kid went by on a bicycle, cards snapping against the spokes.

We should do something, Mary Ann said. Surprise him. Maybe we could take the car over to the house, be waiting out front when he gets back. Wouldn't that be great?

I wouldn't have any way to get home.

Rafe can give you a ride.

Gilbert sat back and watched Mary Ann. She was halfway down her section of the fence. He waited for her to turn and face him. Instead she bent over to work at a spot near the ground. Her hair fell forward, exposing the nape of her neck. Maybe you could invite someone along, Mary Ann said.

Invite someone. What do you mean, a girl?

Sure. It would be nice if you had a girl. It would be perfect.

Gilbert threw the scraper against the fence. He saw Mary Ann freeze. It would *not* be perfect, he said. When she still didn't turn around, he stood and went up the walk and through the house to the kitchen. He paced back and forth. He went to the sink, drank a glass of water, and stood with his hands on the counter. He saw what Mary Ann was thinking of, the two of them sitting in the open car, herself jumping out as Rafe pulled up, the wild embrace. Rafe unshaven, reeking of smoke and nature, a little abashed at all this emotion in front of his father but pleased, too, and amused. And all the while Gilbert looking coolly on, hands in his pockets, ready to say the sly mocking words that would tell Rafe that all was as before. That was how she saw it going. As if nothing had happened.

Mary Ann had just about finished her section when Gilbert came back outside. I'll go get the paint, he told her. I don't think there's much left to scrape on my side, but you can take a look.

She stood and tried to smile. Thank you, she said.

He saw that she had been in tears, and this did not soften him but confirmed him in his purpose.

Mary Ann had already spread out the tarp, pulling one edge under the fence so the drips wouldn't fall on the grass. When Gilbert opened the can she laughed and said, Look! They gave you the wrong color.

No, that's exactly the right color.

But it's *red*. We need white. Like it is now.

You don't want to use white, Mary Ann. Believe me.

She frowned.

Red's the perfect color for this. No offense, but white is the worst choice you could make.

But the house is white.

Exactly, Gilbert said. So are the houses next door. You put a white fence here, what you end up with is complete boredom. It's like being in a hospital, you know what I mean?

I don't know. I guess it is a lot of white.

What the red will do, the red will give some contrast and pick up the bricks in the walk. It's just what you want here.

Well, maybe. The thing is, I don't think I should. Not this time. Next time, maybe, if my dad wants to.

Look, Mary Ann. What your dad wants is for you to use your own head.

Mary Ann squinted at the fence.

You have to trust me on this, okay?

She sucked in her lower lip, then nodded. Okay. If you're sure.

Gilbert dipped his brush. The world's bland enough already, right? Everyone's always talking about the banality of evil—what about the evil of banality?

They painted through the morning and into the afternoon. Every now and then Mary Ann would back off a few steps and take in what they'd done. At first she kept her thoughts to herself. The more they painted, the more she had to say. Toward the end she went out into the street and stood there with her hands on her hips. It's interesting, isn't it? Really different. I see what you mean about picking up the bricks. It's pretty red, though.

It's perfect.

Think my dad'll like it?

Your dad? He'll be crazy about it.

Think so? Gilbert? Really?

Wait till you see his face.

Migraine

*I*t began while she was at work. At the first pang her breath caught and her eyes went wide open. Then it subsided, leaving a faint pressure at the back of her neck. Joyce put her hands on either side of the keyboard and waited. From the cubicles around her she heard the steady click of other keyboards. She knew what was happening to her, knew so well that when the next wave came she felt it not as pain but as dread for what was still to come. Joyce closed down the terminal, then gathered the lab reports and put them in a folder.

She stopped in the doorway of her supervisor's office to say that she was leaving early. Her supervisor made a sympathetic face and offered to call a cab if Joyce didn't feel up to the drive; she could pay for it out of petty cash. "That's what it's there for," she said.

"I'll manage," Joyce told her. She added: "You don't have to whisper."

Joyce did not drive home. Instead she called a taxi from the lobby of the building, as she had intended to do all along. Her supervisor might think that she was giving the money freely, but it wouldn't work out that way.

Whatever people gave you from their overflowing hearts they remembered, and expected you to remember, forever. In Joyce's experience there was no such thing as petty cash.

When she got home she found two cardboard boxes in the living room, filled with her roommate's few belongings. Joyce and Dina had quarreled again, and now Dina was taking the final step in their agreement that she should move out. Joyce looked at the boxes. She considered searching through them, then rejected the idea as beneath her. It was the kind of thing she used to do but had taught herself, with difficulty, to stop doing. She closed her eyes for a moment, swaying slightly from side to side, then crossed the room and turned the television on. A screaming host in a yellow blazer was trying to make himself heard over the delirium of his audience as a big clock ticked away the seconds. Joyce turned the volume off and went into the kitchen to boil some water for tea.

The newspaper was strewn over the countertop, its edges fluttering in the breeze. Dina had left the window open again. Though Joyce kept after her, she refused to take ordinary precautions and shrugged off her carelessness as the unimportant, even lovable consequence of being a free spirit with no material hangups. But Joyce saw through her; she understood that by playing this part Dina had forced the opposite role on her, that of the grasping neurotic. Joyce caught herself acting like this sometimes. But not anymore. All that was over now.

Joyce started the water and went to the window. She rested her elbows on the sill and held her face in her hands, kneading her temples with her fingertips. She pressed harder and harder as the pulse quickened. At the worst moment she went suddenly deaf, as if someone had pushed her head underwater. Then it passed. Joyce heard her own ragged breathing. She heard the scrabble of pigeons' feet on the tile roof and children's voices from the playground of a nearby school, a jackhammer far enough away that its sound was bearable, even companionable, like the distant sound of marching bands in the college town where she had grown up.

Joyce let the breeze cool the sweat from her face. Then she closed the window and began to fill her brewing spoon with chamomile, tilia, and spearmint.

Joyce's eyes were scratchy. Her skin felt damp, and her blouse clung coldly where it had soaked through. She carried the tea to her bedroom and left it steeping on the nightstand while she undressed and sat on the edge of her bed. The room was a mess. Clothes everywhere, hanging from hooks and knobs and bunched on the floor. Newspapers. Suitcases still packed for a visit to Dina's parents, which they'd never made because Joyce got sick. She bent to pick up a shoe, then dropped it and rocked forward onto her feet. She wrapped herself in a terry bathrobe and went to the living room, where, propped up on the sofa, she sipped her tea and watched the silent television.

The tea helped. Not much, really, but it gave Joyce the only influence she had over what was happening to her. Except for Dina's massages, nothing else worked at all. Joyce had taken medicinal baths. She'd gotten drunk and she'd gotten stoned. She had tried every remedy she'd ever heard of, barring the obviously useless ones like breathing through a scuba diver's tank. That suggestion appeared in a newsletter Dina had forced her to subscribe to until Joyce decided that reading about the problem all the time was making it worse instead of better. Also she despised the self-pitying tone of the newsletter, and its spurious implication that readers were not alone in their suffering.

Because they were alone. In fact everyone was alone all

the time, but when you got sick you knew it, and that was a lot of what suffering was—knowing.

Joyce drank off the last of her tea. She set the mug down on the floor and stared at Dina's boxes. Almadén: Dina must have brought them from the liquor store. The tops were open. A white mohair sweater lay on top of one box, a jumble of bottles and tubes on top of the other. Joyce leaned back. Even with her eyes closed she could sense the flickering of the television as the camera jumped from host to contestants, contestants to host. The apartment was profoundly quiet.

It was good to be alone. Really alone, without other people around to let you imagine that your life had mingled with theirs. That never was true. Even together, people were as solitary as cows in a field chewing their own cud.

You couldn't enter the life of another person even when you wanted to. Back in August Joyce and Dina had a friend over for dinner, and in the course of the evening she told a story about a couple they all knew who'd recently been injured in a peculiar accident. A waterbed with a fat guy on it had crashed through their ceiling while they were watching TV and landed right on top of them. It was a miracle they weren't killed—not that this view of the episode would comfort them much, considering the hurts they did end up with: a broken collarbone for one, a sprained neck and concussion for the other. Joyce and Dina shook their heads when their friend came to the end of this story. They looked down at their plates. Joyce managed to keep her jaw clenched until Dina began snorting, and then all three of them let go. They howled. They couldn't stop. Joyce got so short of breath she had to push her chair back and lower her head between her knees.

And yet she had known these women. Their pain should have meant something to her. But even now, in pain herself, she couldn't feel theirs, or come any closer than thinking that she ought to feel it. And the same would be true if the waterbed had fallen on her and Dina instead of on them. Even if it had killed her they would have laughed, then afterward regretted their laughter as she had regretted hers. They'd have gone on about their business, remembering her less and less often, and always with a sudden helpless smile like the one she felt on her own lips right now.

The effects of the tea were wearing off. Joyce raised her head from the pillows and slowly sat up. She stared at the boxes again, then looked at the television. A man was smiling steadfastly while the woman next to him emptied a container of white goo over his head.

Joyce pushed herself up. She went to the kitchen and filled the kettle with fresh water, then leaned against the counter. The pulse was getting stronger again; each time it struck she dipped her head slightly, as if she were nodding off. She entered another period of deafness. When she came out of it the kettle-top was rattling; beads of water rolled down the sides, hissing against the burner. Joyce refilled the brewing spoon, poured water into her cup, and carried it back to the living room. She knelt between Dina's boxes and began searching through the one with the sweater on top.

Beneath the sweater were some photographs that Dina had kept in her vanity mirror, stuck between the glass and the frame. A whole series of her brother and his family, the two daughters getting taller from picture to picture, their sweet round faces growing thin and wary. A formal portrait of Dina's parents. Several snapshots of Joyce. Joyce glanced through these pictures and put them aside. She sat back on her heels. She drew a deep, purposeful breath and held her head erect, the very picture of a woman who has just managed to get the better of herself after a moment's weakness. The refrigerator motor kicked on. Joyce could hear bottles tinkling against each other. Joyce took another breath, then leaned forward again and continued to unpack the box.

Clothes. Shoes. A blow-dryer. Finally, at the bottom, Dina's books: *Chariots of the Gods*, *The Inner Game of Tennis*, *Many Mansions*, *In Search of Bigfoot*, *The No-Sweat Workout*, and *The Bhagavad-Gita*. Joyce opened *In Search of Bigfoot* and flipped through the illustrations. These included a voice-graph taken from a hidden microphone, the plaster cast of a large foot with surprisingly thin, fingerlike toes, and a blurry picture of the monster itself walking across a clearing with its arms swinging casually at its sides. Joyce repacked the box. No wonder her brain was eroding. Dina had so much junk in her head that just having a conversation with her was like being sandblasted.

Once Dina moved out, Joyce was going to get her mind back in shape. She had a list of books she intended to read. She was going to keep a journal and take some night classes in philosophy. Joyce had done well in her philosophy survey course back in college, so well that when her professor returned the final paper he attached a note of thanks to Joyce for helping to make the class such a pleasure to teach.

Not that Joyce thought of becoming a professional philosopher. But she felt alive when she talked about ideas, and she still remembered the calm certainty with which her professor stalked the beliefs of his students down to their origins in superstition and hearsay and mere emotion. He was famous for making people cry. Joyce became adept at this kind of argument herself. She had moments of the purest clarity when she could feel herself striking closer and closer to the truth, while observing with amused detachment the panic of some classmate in danger of forfeiting an illusion. Joyce had not felt so clear about anything since, because she had been involved with other people, and other people muddied the water. What with their needs and their demands and their feelings, their almighty anxieties to be tended to eight or nine times a day, you ended up telling so many lies that in time you forgot what the truth sounded like. But Joyce wasn't that far gone—not yet. Alone, she could begin to read again, to think, to see things as they were. Alone, she could be as cold and hard as the truth demanded. No more false cheer. No pretense of intimacy. No lies.

Another thing. No more TV. Joyce had bought it only as a way of keeping Dina quiet, but that would no longer be necessary. She picked up the remote control, watched the rest of a commercial for pickup trucks, then turned the set off. The blank screen made her uncomfortable. Jumpy, almost as if it were watching her. Joyce put the remote control back on the coffee table and began to unpack the other box.

Halfway down, between two towels, she found what she was looking for. A pair of scissors, fine German scissors that belonged to her. Joyce hadn't known she was looking for them, but when her fingers touched the blades she almost laughed out loud. Dina had taken her scissors. Deliberately. There was no chance of a mistake, because these scissors were unique. They had cunning brass handles that formed the outline of a duck's head when closed, and the blades were engraved with German words that meant "For my dear Karin from her loving father." Joyce had found the scissors at an antique store on Post Street, and from the moment she brought them home Dina had been fascinated by them. She borrowed them so often that Joyce suspected her of inventing work just to have an excuse to use them. And now she'd stolen them.

Joyce held the scissors above the box and snicked them open and shut several times. Wasn't this an eye-opener, though. Little Miss Free Spirit, Miss Unencumbered by Worldly Goods would rather steal than live without a pair of scissors. She was a thief—a hypocrite and a thief.

Joyce put the scissors down beside the remote control. She pushed the heel of her hand hard against her forehead. For the first time that day she felt tired. With luck she might even be able to sleep for a while.

Joyce slid the scissors back between the towels and repacked the box. Dina could have them. There was no point in saying anything to her—she'd only feign surprise and say it was an accident—and no way for Joyce to mention the scissors without revealing that she had searched the boxes. Dina could keep the damn things, and as time went by it would begin to dawn on her, so many months, so many years later, that Joyce must know she'd stolen them; but still Joyce would not mention them, not in her Christmas cards or the friendly calls she'd make on Dina's birthday or the postcards she'd send from the various countries she planned to visit. In the end Dina would know that Joyce had pardoned her and made a gift of the scissors, and then, for the first time, she would begin to understand the kind of person Joyce really was, and how wrong she had been about her—how blind and unfeeling. At last she would know what she had lost.

When Joyce woke up, Dina was standing beside the sofa looking down at her. A few bars of pale light lay across the rug and the wall; the rest of the room was in shadow. Joyce tried to raise her head. It felt like a stone. She settled back again.

"I knew it," Dina said.

Joyce waited. When Dina just kept looking at her, she asked, "Knew what?"

"Guess." Dina turned away and went into the kitchen.

Joyce heard her running water into the kettle. Joyce called, "Are you referring to the fact that I'm sick?"

Dina didn't answer.

"It doesn't concern you," Joyce said.

Dina came to the kitchen door. "Don't do this, Joyce. At least be honest about what's happening, okay?"

"Pretend I'm not here," Joyce said. "This has nothing to do with you."

Dina shook her head. "I just can't believe you're doing this." She went back in the kitchen.

"Doing *what*?" Joyce asked. "I'm lying here on the couch. Is that what I'm doing?"

"You know," Dina said. She leaned into the doorway again and said, "Stop playing head games."

"Head games," Joyce repeated. "Jesus Mary and Joseph."

Dina took a step into the living room. "It isn't fair, Joyce."

Joyce turned onto her side. She lay motionless, listening to Dina bang around in the kitchen.

"I'm not stupid!" Dina yelled.

"Nobody said you were."

Dina came into the living room carrying two cups. She set one down on the coffee table where Joyce could reach it and carried the other to the easy chair.

"Thanks," Joyce said. She sat up slowly, nodding with dizziness. She picked up the tea and held it against her chest, letting the fragrant steam warm her face.

Dina leaned forward and blew into her cup. "You look horrible," she said.

Joyce smiled.

The two of them drank their tea, watching each other over the cups. "I'm going crazy," Dina said. "I can't plan a trip to the beach without you pulling this stuff."

"Ignore me," Joyce told her.

"That's what you always say. I'm leaving, Joyce. Maybe not now, but someday."

"Leave now," Joyce said.

"Do you really want me to?"

"If you're going to leave, leave now."

"You look just awful. It really hurts, doesn't it?"

"Pretend I'm not here," Joyce said.

"But I *can't*. You know I can't. That's what's so unfair. I can't just walk out when you're hurting like this."

"Dina."

"What?"

Joyce shook her head. "Nothing. Nothing."

Dina said, "Damn you, Joyce."

"You should leave," Joyce said.

"I'm going to. That's a promise. Don't ever say you didn't have fair warning."

Joyce nodded.

Dina stood and picked up one of the boxes. "I heard a great Polack joke today."

"Not now," Joyce said. "It would kill me."

Dina carried the box to her bedroom and came back for the other one, the one with the scissors. It was bulkier than the first and she had trouble getting a grip on it. "Damn you," she said to Joyce. "I can't believe I'm doing this."

Joyce finished her tea. She crossed her arms and leaned forward until her head was almost touching her knees. From Dina's bedroom she could hear the sound of drawers being yanked open and slammed shut. Then there was silence, and when Joyce raised her head Dina was standing over her again.

"Poor old Joyce," she said.

Joyce shrugged.

"Move over," Dina said. She arranged herself at the end of the sofa and said, "Okay." Joyce lay down again, her head in Dina's lap. Dina looked down at her. She brushed back a lock of Joyce's hair.

"Head games," Joyce said, and laughed.

"Shut up," Dina said.

Dina shifted a little to one side. She laid one hand on each side of Joyce's face, fingers along her cheeks, and began to push her thumbs against Joyce's temples. She moved her thumbs back and forth in tight circles, steadily increasing the pressure. At first the rhythm was fluid and almost imperceptible, but as it grew more definite Dina began humming to herself. Joyce closed her eyes. She felt her eyelids flutter nervously, then grow still. She heard the newspaper rustle in the kitchen. She felt Dina purring her song. She felt the softness of Dina's thighs, and the warmth they gave off. Dina's hands were warm against her cheeks. Joyce reached up and covered them with her own hands, as if to keep them there.

The Chain

*B*rian Gold was at the top of the hill when the dog attacked. A big black wolf-like animal attached to a chain, it came flying off a back porch and tore through its yard into the park, moving easily in spite of the deep snow, making for Gold's daughter. He waited for the chain to pull the dog up short; the dog kept coming. Gold plunged down the hill, shouting as he went. Snow and wind deadened his voice. Anna's sled was almost at the bottom of the slope. Gold had raised the hood of her parka against the needling gusts, and he knew that she could not hear him or see the dog racing toward her. He was conscious of the dog's speed and of his own dreamy progress, the weight of his gumboots, the clinging trap of crust beneath the new snow. His overcoat flapped at his knees. He screamed one last time as the dog made its lunge, and at that moment Anna flinched away and the dog caught her shoulder instead of her face. Gold was barely halfway down the hill, arms pumping, feet sliding in the boots. He seemed to be running in place, held at a fixed, unbridgeable distance as the dog dragged Anna backwards off the sled, shaking her like a doll. Gold threw himself down the hill helplessly, then the distance vanished and he was there.

The sled was overturned, the snow churned up; the dog had marked this ground as its own. It still had Anna by the shoulder. Gold heard the rage boiling in its gut. He saw the tensed hindquarters and the flattened ears and the red gleam of gum under the wrinkled snout. Anna was on her back, her face bleached and blank, staring at the sky. She had never looked so small. Gold seized the chain and yanked at it, but could get no purchase in the snow. The dog only snarled more fiercely and started shaking Anna again. She didn't make a sound. Her silence made Gold go hollow and cold. He flung himself onto the dog and hooked his arm under its neck and pulled back hard. Still the dog wouldn't let go. Gold felt its heat and the profound rumble of its will. With his other hand he tried to pry the jaw loose. His gloves turned slippery with drool; he couldn't get a grip. Gold's mouth was next to the dog's ear. He said, "Let go, damn you," and then he took the ear between his teeth and bit down with everything he had. He heard a yelp and something cracked against his nose, knocking him backwards. When he pushed himself up the dog was running for home, jerking its head from side to side, scattering flecks of blood on the snow.

"The whole thing took maybe sixty seconds," Gold said. "Maybe less. But it went on forever." He'd told the story many times now, and always mentioned this. He knew it was trite to marvel at the way time could stretch and stall, but he was unable not to. Nor could he stop himself from repeating that it was a "miracle"—the radiologist's word—that Anna hadn't been crippled or disfigured, or even killed; and that her doctor did not understand how she'd escaped damage to her bones and nerves. Though badly bruised, her skin hadn't even been broken.

Gold loved his daughter's face. He loved her face as a thing in itself, to be wondered at, studied. Yet after the attack he couldn't look at Anna in the same way. He kept seeing the dog lunge at her, and himself stuck forever on that hill; then his heart began to kick, and he grew taut and restless and angry. He didn't want to think about the dog anymore—he wanted it out of the picture. It should be put down. It was crazy, a menace, and it was still there, waiting to tear into some other kid, because the police refused to do anything.

"They won't do a thing," he said. "Nothing."

He was going through the whole story again with his cousin Tom Rourke on a Sunday afternoon, a week after the attack. Gold had called him the night it happened, but the part about the police was new, and Rourke got all worked up just as Gold expected. His cousin had an exacting, irritable sense of justice, and a ready store of loyal outrage that Gold had drawn on ever since they were boys. He had been alone in his anger for a week now and wanted some company. Though his wife claimed to be angry too, she hadn't seen what he had seen. The dog was an abstraction to her, and she wasn't one to brood anyway.

What was their excuse? Rourke wanted to know. What reason did the cops give for their complete and utter worthlessness?

"The chain," Gold said. "They said—this is the really beautiful part—they said that since the dog was chained up, no law was broken."

"But the dog *wasn't* chained up, right?"

"He was, but the chain reaches into the park. I mean way in—a good thirty, forty feet."

"By that logic, he could be on a chain ten miles long and legally chew up the whole fucking town."

"Exactly."

Rourke got up and went to the picture window. He stood close to the glass and glowered at the falling snow. "What is it with Nazis and dogs? They've got a real thing going, ever notice that?" Still looking out the window, he said, "Have you talked to a lawyer?"

"Day before yesterday."

"What'd he say?"

"She. Kate Stiller. Said the police were full of shit. Then she told me to forget it. According to her, the dog'll die of old age before we ever get near a courtroom."

"There's the legal system for you, Brian me boy. They'll give you all the justice you want, as long as it's up the ass."

There was a loud thump on the ceiling. Anna was playing upstairs with Rourke's boy, Michael. Both men raised their eyes and waited, and when no one screamed Gold said, "I don't know why I even bothered to call her. I don't have the money to pay for a lawyer."

"You know what happened," Rourke said. "The cop who took the complaint fucked it up, and now the others are covering for him. So, you want to take him out?"

"The *cop*?"

"I was thinking of the dog."

"You mean kill the dog?"

Rourke just looked at Gold.

"Is that what you're saying? Kill the dog?"

Rourke grinned, but he still didn't say anything.

"How?"

"How do you want?"

"Christ, Tom, I can't believe I'm talking like this."

"But you are." Rourke shoved the naugahyde ottoman with his foot until it was facing Gold, then sat on it and leaned forward, so close their knees were touching. "No poison or glass. That's chickenshit, I wouldn't do that to my worst enemy. Take him out clean."

"Christ, Tom." Gold tried to laugh.

"You can use my Remington, scope him in from the hill. Or if you want, get up close with the 12-gauge or the .44 magnum. You ever fired a pistol?"

"No."

"Better forget the magnum, then."

"I can't do this."

"Sure you can."

"They'll know it was me. I've been raising hell about that dog all week. Who do you think they're going to come after when it suddenly shows up with a hole in its head?"

Rourke sucked in his cheeks. "Point taken," he said. "Okay, you can't do it. But I sure as hell can."

"No. Forget it, Tom."

"You and Mary go out for the night. Have dinner at Chez Nicole or Pauly's, someplace small where they'll remember you. By the time you get home it's all over and you're clean as a whistle."

Gold finished his beer.

"We've got to take care of business, Brian. If we don't, nobody will."

"Maybe if I did it. *Maybe.* Having you do it—that just doesn't feel right."

"What about that dog still running wild after what it did to Anna? Does that feel right?" When Gold didn't answer, Rourke shook his knee. "Did you really bite the mutt's ear?"

"I didn't have any choice."

"You bite it off?"

"No."

"But you drew blood, right? You tasted blood."

"I got some in my mouth, yes. I couldn't help it."

"It tasted good, didn't it? Come on, Brian, don't bullshit me, it tasted good."

"There was a certain satisfaction," Gold said.

"You want to do what's right," Rourke said. "I appreciate that. I value that. It's your call, okay? But the offer stands."

Rourke produced the crack about Nazis and dogs not from deep reflection, Gold knew, but because to call people Nazis was his first response to any vexation or slight. Once he'd heard Rourke say it, though, Gold could not forget it. The picture that came to mind was one he'd pondered before: a line of frenzied dogs harrying Jews along a railway platform.

Gold was Jewish on his father's side, but his parents split up when he was young, and he'd been raised Catholic by his mother. His name didn't suit him; he sensed it made him seem ridiculous. When you heard Gold, what else could you think of but gold? With that name he should be a rich sharpie, not a mackerel-snapper with a dying business. The black kids who came into his video store were unmistakably of that opinion. They had a mock-formal way of saying "Mr. *Gold*," drawing out the word as if it were the precious substance itself. Finding themselves a little short on the rental fee, some of them weren't above asking him to make up the difference out of his own deep pockets, and acting amazed if he refused. The rusty Toyota he kept parked out front was a puzzle to them, a conversation piece; they couldn't figure out why, with all his money, he didn't get himself a decent set of wheels. One night, standing at the counter with her friends, a girl suggested that Gold kept his Cadillac at home because he was afraid the brothers would steal it. They'd been goofing on him, just messing around, but when she said this everyone went silent as if a hard truth had been spoken.

Cadillac. What else?

After years of estrangement Gold had returned to the Catholic church, and went weekly to Mass to sustain his fragile faith, but he understood that in the eyes of the world he was a Jew. He had never known what to make of that. There were things he saw in himself that he thought of as Jewish, traits not conspicuous among the mostly Irish boys he'd grown up with, including his cousins. Bookishness, patience, a taste for classical music and complicated moralizing, aversion to alcohol and violence. All this he found acceptable. But he had certain other tendencies, less dear to him, that he also suspected of being Jewish. Corrosive self-mockery. Bouts of almost paralyzing skepticism. Physical awkwardness. A disposition toward passivity, even surrender, in the face of bullying people and oppressive circumstances. Gold knew that these ideas of Jewishness were also held by anti-Semites, and he resisted their influence, without much success.

In the already familiar picture that Rourke had conjured up, of Jews being herded by dogs, Gold sensed an instance of the resignation that he disliked in himself. He knew it was unfair to blame people for not fighting an evil that their very innocence made them incapable of imagining, yet even while admitting that they were brutalized and starved and in shock, he couldn't help but wonder: Why didn't one of them hit a guard—grab his gun—take some of the bastards with him? *Do* something? Even in his awareness of the terrible injustice of this question, he'd never really laid it to rest.

And with that old image vivid in his thoughts, it seemed to Gold that the question had now been put to him. Why didn't he do something? His own daughter had been savaged by just such a dog, a flinch away from having her face torn off. He had seen its insanity, felt its furious will to hurt. And it was still out there, lying in wait, because no one, himself included, would do what needed to be done.

He could not escape the consciousness of his own inaction. In the days following his conversation with Rourke, it became intolerable. No matter where he was, at home or in the store, he was also on that hill, unable to move or speak, watching the dog come at Anna with murder in its heart and the chain gliding behind like an infinite black snake.

He drove by the park late one day and stopped across the street from the house where the dog's owners lived. It was a Colonial with a line of dormer windows, a big expensive house like most of the others around the park. Gold thought he could guess why the police had been so docile. This wasn't a shooting gallery, a crib for perpetrators and scofflaws. The deep thunk of the brass knocker against the great green door, the glittering chandelier in the foyer, the Cinderella sweep of the staircase with its monumental newel post and gleaming rail—all this would tell you that the law was among friends here. Of course a dog needed room to roam. If people let their kids go tearing off every which way, they'd have to live with the consequences. Some folks were just natural-born whiners.

Though Gold despaired of the police, he believed he understood them. He did not understand the people who'd allowed this to happen. They had never called to apologize, or even to ask how Anna was. They seemed not to care that their dog was a killer. Gold had driven here with some notion of sitting down with them, helping them see what they ought to do—as if they'd even let him in the door. What a patsy!

He called Rourke that night and told him to go ahead.

Rourke was hot on the idea of Gold taking Mary out for dinner—his treat—on the big night. He had a theatrical conception of the event, which seemed to include the two of them toasting him with champagne while he did whatever he meant to do.

Gold refused the offer. Mary didn't know what they were up to, and he couldn't sit across a table from her for three hours, even as the deed was being done, without telling. She wouldn't like it, but she wouldn't be able to stop it; the knowledge would only be a burden to her. Gold employed a graduate student named Simms who covered the store at night, except for Tuesdays, when he had a seminar. Though Rourke was disappointed by Gold's humdrum dramaturgy, he assented: Tuesday night it was.

More snow fell that morning, followed by an ice storm. The streets and sidewalks were still glazed by nightfall and business was slow. As always Gold had a new release playing in the monitor above the counter, but he couldn't follow the plot through the frantic cutting and ugly music, so he stopped it halfway through and didn't bother to put in another. That left the store oddly quiet. Maybe for this reason his customers didn't linger in the usual way, shooting the breeze with Gold and one another. They made their selections, paid and left. He tried to read the paper. At eight-thirty Anna called to say she'd won a poster contest at school. After she hung up, Gold witnessed a fight in front of the Domino's across the street. Two men, drunk or drugged, had a shouting match, and one of them took a clumsy swing at the other. They grappled and fell down together on the ice. A deliveryman and one of the cooks came outside and helped them up, then walked them off in different directions. Gold microwaved the chili left over from Sunday dinner. He ate slowly, watching the sluggish procession of cars and the hunched, gingerly trudge of people past his window. Mary had laid on the cumin with a free hand, which was just how Gold liked it. His forehead grew damp with sweat, and he took off his sweater. The baseboard heaters ticked. The long fluorescent lights buzzed overhead.

Rourke called just before ten, when Gold was closing up. "Scooter has buried his last bone," he said.

"Scooter?"

"That was his name."

"I wish you hadn't told me."

"I got his collar for you—a little memento."

"For Christ's sake, Tom."

"Don't worry, you're clear."

"Just don't tell me any more," Gold said. "I'm afraid I'll say too much when the police come by."

"They're not gonna come by. The way I fixed things, they won't even know what happened." He coughed. "It had to be done, Brian."

"I guess."

"No guessing about it. But I've gotta say, it wasn't anything I'd want to do again."

"I'm sorry, Tom. I should've done it myself."

"It wasn't any fun, I'll tell you that." Rourke fell silent. Gold could hear him breathing. "I about froze my ass off. I thought they'd never let the damned beast out."

"I won't forget it," Gold said.

"*De nada*. It's over. Go in peace."

In late March, Rourke called Gold with a story of his own. He'd been gassing up on Erie Boulevard when a BMW backed away from the air hose and put a crease in his door. He yelled at the driver, a black man wearing sunglasses and a knit cap. The driver ignored him. He looked straight ahead and drove off across the lot into the road, but not before Rourke got a good look at his license plate. It was a vanity tag, easy to remember—SCUSE ME. Rourke called the police, who tracked the driver down and ticketed him for leaving the scene of an accident.

So far, so good. Then it turned out the driver didn't have insurance. Rourke's company agreed to cover most of the bill—eight hundred bucks for a lousy dent!—but that still left him with the three-hundred-dollar deductible. Rourke figured Mr. SCUSE ME should make up the difference. His insurance agent gave him the man's name and particulars, and Rourke started calling him. He called twice at reasonable hours, after dinner, but both times the woman who answered said he wasn't in and gave Rourke the number of a club on Townsend, where he got an answering machine. Though he left clear messages, he heard nothing back. Finally Rourke called the first number at seven in the morning and got the man himself, Mr. Vick Barnes.

"That's V-I-C-K," Rourke said. "Ever notice the way they do that with their names? You shorten Victor, you get Vic, right? V-I-C. So where does the fucking K come from? Or take Sean, S-E-A-N. Been spelled like that for about five hundred years. But not them, they've gotta spell it S-H-A-W-N. Like they have a right to that name in the first place."

"What did he say?"

"Gave me a lot of mouth, natch. First he gets indignant that I woke him up, then he says he's already been through all this shit with the police, and he doesn't believe he hit anybody anyway. Then he hangs up on me."

Rourke said he knew better than to call back; he wasn't going to get anywhere with this guy. Instead he went to the club, Jack's Shady Corner, where it turned out Mr. Vick Barnes worked as a deejay, and no doubt retailed dope on the side. All the deejays did. Where else would he get the dough for a new Beamer? But Rourke had to admit he was quite the pro, our Mr. Barnes, nice mellow voice, good line of patter. Rourke had a couple beers and watched the dancers, then went looking for the car.

It wasn't in the lot. Rourke poked around and found it off by itself in a little nook behind the club, where it wouldn't get run into by drunks. He was going back tonight to give Mr. Vick Barnes a taste of his own medicine, plus a little extra for the vigorish.

"You can't," Gold said. "They'll know it was you."

"Let 'em prove it."

Gold had understood from the start where this story was taking him, even if Rourke hadn't. When he said "I'll do it," he felt as if he was reading the words from a script.

"No need, Brian. I got it covered."

"Wait a minute. Just hang on." Gold put the receiver down and took care of an old woman who was renting *The Sound of Music*. Then he picked it up and said, "They'll bust you for sure."

"Look, I can't let this guy fuck me over and just walk away. Next thing, everybody in town'll be lining up to give me the wood."

"I told you, I'll handle it. Not tonight—there's a talent show at school. Thursday."

"You sure, Brian?"

"I said I'd do it. Didn't I just say I'd do it?"

"Only if you really want to. Okay? Don't feel like you have to."

Rourke stopped by the store Thursday afternoon with instructions and equipment: two gallons of Olympic redwood stain to pour over the BMW, a hunting knife to slash the tires and score the paint, and a crowbar to break the windshield. Gold was to exercise extreme caution. He should work fast. He should leave his car running, and pointed in the direction of a clear exit. If for any reason things didn't look right he should leave immediately.

They loaded the stuff in the trunk of Gold's car.

"Where are you going to be?" Gold asked.

"Chez Nicole's. Same place you'd have gone if you had any class."

"I had a good sole meunière last time I was there."

"Prime rib for this bad boy. Rare. Taste of blood, eh, Brian?"

Gold watched him drive off. It was a warm day, the third in a row. Last week's snow had turned gray and was offering up its holdings of beer cans and dog turds. The gutters overflowed with melt, and the sun shone on the wet pavement and the broken glass in front of Domino's, which had abruptly closed three weeks earlier. Rourke's brake lights flashed. He stopped and backed up. Gold waited while the electric window descended, then leaned toward the car.

"Careful, Brian, okay?"

"You know me."

"Don't get caught. I have to say, that's something you definitely want to avoid."

Gold drove to the club at eleven-thirty, with the idea that there wouldn't be much coming and going at that hour on a weeknight. The casual drinkers would already be home, the serious crowd settling in for the duration. A dozen or so cars were scattered across the lot. Gold backed into a space as close to the rear of the building as he could get. He turned the engine off and looked around, then popped the trunk, took the crowbar and moved into the shadows around back. The BMW was parked where Rourke said it would be, in the short driveway between the alley and the dumpster.

Gold had no intention of using the stain or the knife. Rourke had suffered a dent; that was no reason to destroy a man's car. One good dent in return would even things up between Rourke and Barnes, and settle his own debt in the bargain. If Rourke wanted more, he was strictly on his own.

Gold walked around the car—a beautiful machine, a gleaming black 328 with those special wheels that gang members were supposedly killing each other over. The dealership where Gold took his Toyota for repairs also had the local BMW boutique, and he always paid a visit to the showroom while he waited. He liked to open and close the doors, sit in the leather seats and work the gears, compare options and prices. Fully loaded, this model ran in the neighborhood of forty grand. Gold couldn't imagine Mr. Vick Barnes qualifying for that kind of a loan on a deejay's salary, so he must have paid in cash. Rourke was right. He was dealing.

Gold hefted the crowbar. He felt the driving pulse of the music through the club walls, heard the vocalist—he wouldn't call him a singer—shouting along with menace and complaint. It was a strange thing. You sold drugs to your own people, ruined their neighborhoods, turned their children into prostitutes and thugs, and you became a big shot. A man of property and respect. But try to run a modest business, bring something good into their community, and you were a bloodsucking parasite and a Child of Satan. Mr. *Gold*. He smacked the bar against his palm. He was thinking maybe he'd do a little something with that knife after all. The stain too. He could find uses for the stain.

A woman laughed in the parking lot and a man answered in a low voice. Gold crouched behind the dumpster and waited until their headlights raked the darkness and vanished. His hand was tight around the metal. He could feel his own rage, and distrusted it. Only a fool acted out of anger. No, he would do exactly what was fair, what he had decided on before coming here.

Gold walked around to the driver's side of the BMW. He held the crowbar with both hands and touched the curved end against the door at bumper height, where Rourke's car would have been hit. He adjusted his feet. He touched the door again, then cocked the crowbar like a bat and swung it with everything he had, knowing just as the act passed beyond recall how absolutely he had betrayed himself. The shock of the blow raced up his arms. He dropped the crowbar and left it where it fell.

Victor Emmanuel Barnes found it there three hours later. He knelt and ran his hand along the jagged cleft in the car door, flecks of paint curling away under his fingertips. He knew exactly who had done this. He picked up the crowbar, tossed it on the passenger seat, and drove straight to the apartment building where Devereaux lived. As he sped through the empty streets he howled and pounded the dashboard. He stopped in a shriek of brakes and seized the crowbar and ran up the stairs to Devereaux's door. He pounded the door with his fist. *I told you next week, you motherfucker. I told you next week.* He demanded to be let in. He heard voices, but when no one answered him he cursed them and began working at the door with the crowbar. It creaked and strained. Then it gave and Barnes staggered into the apartment, yelling for Devereaux.

But Devereaux wasn't home. His sixteen-year-old nephew Marcel was spending the night on the couch after helping Devereaux's little girl write an essay. He stood facing the door while Barnes jimmied it, his aunt and cousins and grandmother gathered behind him at the end of the hall, shaking and clinging to one another. When Barnes stumbled bellowing inside, Marcel tried to push him back out. They struggled. Barnes shoved him away and swung the crowbar, catching Marcel right across the temple. The boy's eyes went wide. His mouth opened. He sank to his knees and pitched facedown on the floor. Barnes looked at Marcel, then at the old woman coming toward him. "Oh Jesus," he said, and dropped the crowbar and ran down the stairs and outside to his car. He drove to his grandmother's house and told her what had happened, and she held his head in her lap and rocked over him and wept and prayed. Then she called the police.

Marcel's death was on the morning news. Every half hour they ran the story, with pictures of both him and Barnes. Barnes was shown being hustled into a cruiser, Marcel standing before his exhibit at the All-County Science Fair. He had been an honors student at Morris Fields High, a volunteer in the school's Big Brother program, and a past president of the Christian Youth Association. There was no known motive for the attack.

Camera crews from the TV stations followed students from their buses to the school doors, asking about Marcel and getting close-ups of the most distraught. At the beginning of second period, the principal came on the p.a. system and said that crisis counselors were available for those who wished to speak to them. Any students who felt unable to continue with their classes that day were to be excused.

Garvey Banks looked over at his girlfriend, Tiffany. Neither of them had known Marcel, but it was nice out and there wasn't anything happening at school except people crying and carrying on. When he nodded toward the door, she smiled in that special way of hers and gathered her books and collected a pass from the teacher. Garvey waited a few minutes, then followed her outside.

They walked up to Bickel Park and sat on a bench over-
looking the pond. Two old white ladies were throwing
bread to the ducks. The wet grass steamed in the sun.
Tiffany put her head on Garvey's shoulder and hummed to
herself. Garvey wanted to feel sad over that boy getting
killed, but it was good being warm like this and close to
Tiffany.

They sat on the bench in the sun. They didn't talk. They
hardly ever talked. Tiffany liked to look at things and be
quiet in herself. Pretty soon they'd rent a movie and go
over to Garvey's. They'd kiss. They wouldn't take any
chances, but they'd make each other happy. All of that was
going to happen, and Garvey was glad to wait for it.

After a while Tiffany stopped humming. "Ready, Gar?"

"Ready."

They stopped in at Gold's Video and Garvey took *Breakfast at Tiffany's* off the shelf. They'd rented it the first time
because of the title, then it became their favorite movie.
Someday, they were going to live in New York City and
know all kinds of people—that was for sure.

Mr. Gold was slow writing up the receipt. He looked
sick. He counted out Garvey's change and said, "Why
aren't you kids in school?"

Garvey felt cornered, and decided to blow a little smoke
at the man. "Friend of mine got killed," he said.

"You knew him? You knew Marcel Foley?"

"Yes sir. From way back."

"What was he like?"

"Marcel? Hey, Marcel was the best. You got a problem,
you took it to Marcel. You know, trouble with your girlfriend or whatever. Trouble at home. Trouble with a friend.
Marcel had this thing, right, Tiff?—he could bring people
together. He just had this easy way and he talked to you
like you were important, like everybody's important. He

could get people to come together, know what I'm saying? Come together and get on with it. *Peacemaker.* Marcel was a peacemaker. And that's the best thing you can be."

"Yes," Mr. Gold said. "It is." He put his hands on the counter and lowered his head.

Then Garvey saw that he was grieving, and it came to him how unfair a thing it was that Marcel Foley had been struck down with his life still before him, all his sunny days stolen away. It was wrong, and Garvey knew that it would not end there. He touched Mr. Gold's shoulder. "That man'll get his," he said. "He'll get what's coming to him. Count on it."

Smorgasbord

A prep school in March is like a ship in the doldrums." Our history master said this, as if to himself, while we were waiting for the bell to ring after class. He stood by the window and tapped the glass with his ring in a dreamy, abstracted way meant to make us think he'd forgotten we were there. We were supposed to get the impression that when we weren't around he turned into someone interesting, someone witty and profound, who uttered impromptu bon mots and had a poetic vision of life.

The bell rang.

I went to lunch. The dining hall was almost empty, because it was a free weekend and most of the boys had gone to New York, or home, or to their friends' homes, as soon as their last class let out. About the only ones left were foreigners and scholarship students like me and a few other untouchables of various stripes. The school had laid on a nice lunch for us, cheese soufflé, but the portions were small and I went back to my room still hungry. I was always hungry.

Sleety rain fell past my window. The snow on the quad

looked grimy; it had melted above the underground heating pipes, exposing long brown lines of mud.

I couldn't get to work. On the next floor down someone kept playing "Mack the Knife." That one song incessantly repeating itself made the dorm seem not just empty but abandoned, as if those who had left were never coming back. I cleaned my room, then tried to read. I looked out the window. I sat down at my desk and studied the new picture my girlfriend had sent me, unable to imagine her from it; I had to close my eyes to do that, and then I could see her, her solemn eyes and the heavy white breasts she would gravely let me hold sometimes, but not kiss. Not yet, anyway. But I had a promise. That summer, as soon as I got home, we were going to become lovers. "Become lovers." That was what she'd said, very deliberately, listening to the words as she spoke them. All year I had repeated them to myself to take the edge off my loneliness and the fits of lust that made me want to scream and drive my fists through walls. We were going to become lovers that summer, and we were going to be lovers all through college, true to each other even if we ended up thousands of miles apart again, and after college we were going to marry and join the Peace Corps and do something together that would help people. This was our plan. Back in September, the night before I left for school, we wrote it all down along with a lot of other specifics concerning our future: number of children (6), their names, the kinds of dogs we would own, a sketch of our perfect house. We sealed the paper in a bottle and buried it in her backyard. On our golden anniversary we'd dig it up and show it to our children and grandchildren to prove that dreams can come true.

I was writing her a letter when Crosley came to my room. Crosley was a science whiz. He won the science prize every year and spent his summers working as an intern in different laboratories. He was also a fanatical weight lifter. His arms were so knotty he had to hold them out from his sides as he walked, as if he was carrying buckets. Even his features seemed muscular. His face had a permanent flush. Crosley lived down the hall by himself in one of the only singles in the school. He was said to be a thief; that supposedly was the reason he'd ended up without a roommate. I didn't know if it was true, and I tried to avoid forming an opinion on the matter, but whenever we passed each other I felt embarrassed and looked away.

Crosley leaned in the door and asked me how things were.

I said okay.

He stepped inside and gazed around the room, tilting his head to read my roommate's pennants and the titles of our books. I was uneasy. I said, "So what can I do for you?" not meaning to sound as cold as I did but not exactly regretting it either.

He caught my tone and smiled. It was the kind of smile you put on when you pass a group of people you suspect are talking about you. It was his usual expression.

He said, "You know García, right?"

"García? Sure. I think so."

"You know him," Crosley said. "He runs around with Hidalgo and those guys. He's the tall one."

"Sure," I said. "I know who García is."

"Well, his stepmother is in New York for a fashion show or something, and she's going to drive up and take him out to dinner tonight. She told him to bring along some friends. You want to come?"

"What about Hidalgo and the rest of them?"

"They're at some kind of polo deal in Maryland. Buying horses. Or ponies, I guess it would be."

The notion of someone my age buying ponies to play a game with was so unexpected that I couldn't quite take it in. "Jesus," I said.

Crosley said, "How about it. You want to come?"

I'd never even spoken to García. He was the nephew of a famous dictator, and all his friends were nephews and cousins of other dictators. They lived as they pleased here. Most of them kept cars a few blocks from the campus, though that was completely against the rules. They were cocky and prankish and charming. They moved everywhere in a body, sunglasses pushed up on their heads and jackets slung over their shoulders, twittering all at once like birds, *chinga* this and *chinga* that. The headmaster was completely buffaloed. After Christmas vacation a bunch of them came down with gonorrhea, and all he did was call them in and advise them that they should not be in too great a hurry to lose their innocence. It became a school joke. All you had to do was say the word "innocence" and everyone would crack up.

"I don't know," I said.

"Come on," Crosley said.

"But I don't even know the guy."

"So what? I don't either."

"Then why did he ask you?"

"I was sitting next to him at lunch."

"Terrific," I said. "That explains you. What about me? How come he asked me?"

"He didn't. He told me to bring someone else."

"What, just anybody? Just whoever happened to present himself to your attention?"

Crosley shrugged.

"Sounds great," I said. "Sounds like a recipe for a really memorable evening."

"You got something better to do?" Crosley asked.

"No," I said.

The limousine picked us up under the awning of the head-master's house. The driver, an old man, got out slowly and then slowly adjusted his cap before opening the door for us. García slid in beside the woman in back. Crosley and I sat across from them on seats that pulled down. I caught her scent immediately. For some years afterward I bought perfume for women, and I was never able to find that one.

García erupted into Spanish as soon as the driver closed the door behind me. He sounded angry, spitting words at the woman and gesticulating violently. She rocked back a little, then let loose a burst of her own. I stared openly at her. Her skin was very white. She wore a black cape over a black dress cut just low enough to show her pale throat, and the bones at the base of her throat. Her mouth was red. There was a spot of rouge high on each cheek, not rubbed in to look like real color but left there carelessly, or care-fully, to make you think again how white her skin was. Her teeth were small and sharp-looking, and she bared them in concert with certain gestures and inflections. As she talked her pointed little tongue flicked in and out.

She wasn't a lot older than we were.

She said something definitive and cut her hand through the air. García began to answer her but she said "No!" and chopped the air again. Then she turned and smiled at Crosley and me. It was a completely false smile. She said, "Where would you fellows like to eat?" Her voice sounded lower in English, even a little harsh. She called us "fallows."

"Anywhere is fine with me," I said.

"Anywhere," she repeated. She narrowed her big black eyes and pushed her lips together. I could see that my an-swer disappointed her. She looked at Crosley.

"There's supposed to be a good French restaurant in

Newbury," Crosley said. "Also an Italian place. It depends on what you want."

"No," she said. "It depends on what you want. I am not so hungry."

If García had a preference, he kept it to himself. He sulked in the corner, his round shoulders slumped and his hands between his knees. He seemed to be trying to make a point of some kind.

"There's also a smorgasbord," Crosley said. "If you like smorgasbords."

"Smorgasbord," she said. Obviously the word was new to her. She repeated it to García. He frowned, then answered her in a sullen monotone.

I couldn't believe Crosley had suggested the smorgasbord. It was an egregiously uncouth suggestion. The smorgasbord was where the local fatties went to binge. Football coaches brought whole teams there to bulk up. The food was good enough, and God knows there was plenty of it, all you could eat, actually, but the atmosphere was brutally matter-of-fact. The food was good, though. Big platters of shrimp on crushed ice. Barons of beef. Smoked turkey. No end of food, really.

"You—do you like smorgasbords?" she asked Crosley.

"Yes," he said.

"And you?" she said to me.

I nodded. Then, not to seem wishy-washy, I said, "You bet."

"Smorgasbord," she said. She laughed and clapped her hands. "Smorgasbord!"

Crosley gave directions to the driver and we drove slowly away from the school. She said something to García. He nodded at both of us and gave our names, then looked away again, out the window, where the snowy fields were turning dark. His face was long, his eyes sorrowful as a hound's. He had barely talked to us while we were waiting for the limousine. I didn't know why he was mad at his stepmother, or why he wouldn't talk to us, or why he'd even asked us along, but by now I didn't really care.

She studied us and repeated our names skeptically. "No," she said. She pointed at Crosley and said, "El Blanco." She pointed at me and said, "El Negro." Then she pointed at herself and said, "I am Linda."

"Leen-da," Crosley said. He really overdid it, but she showed her sharp little teeth and said, "*Exactamente.*"

Then she settled back against the seat and pulled her cape close around her shoulders. It soon fell open again. She was restless. She sat forward and leaned back, crossed and recrossed her legs, swung her feet impatiently. She had on black high heels fastened by a thin strap; I could see almost her entire foot. I heard the silky rub of her stockings against each other, and breathed in a fresh breath of her perfume every time she moved. That perfume had a certain effect on me. It didn't reach me as just a smell. It was personal, it seemed to issue from her very privacy. It made the hair bristle on my arms, and sent faint chills across my shoulders and the backs of my knees. Every time she moved I felt a little tug and followed her motion with some slight motion of my own.

When we arrived at the smorgasbord—Swenson's, or Hansen's, some such honest Swede of a name—García refused to get out of the limousine. Linda tried to persuade him, but he shrank back into his corner and would not answer or even look at her. She threw up her hands. "Ah!" she said, and turned away. Crosley and I followed her across the parking lot toward the big red barn. Her dress rustled as she walked. Her heels clicked on the cement.

You could say one thing for the smorgasbord; it wasn't pretentious. This was a real barn, not some quaint fantasy of a barn with butter-churn lamps and little brass ornaments nailed to the walls on strips of leather. The kitchen was at

one end. The rest of it had been left open and filled with pic-
nic tables. Blazing light bulbs hung from the rafters. In the
middle of the barn stood what my English master would
have called "the groaning board"—a great table heaped
with food, every kind of food you could think of, and more.
I'd been there many times and it always gave me a small,
pleasant shock to see how much food there was.

Girls wearing dirndls hustled around the barn, cleaning
up messes, changing tablecloths, bringing fresh platters of
food from the kitchen.

We stood blinking in the sudden light, then followed
one of the waitresses across the floor. Linda walked slowly,
gazing around like a tourist. Several men looked up from
their food as she passed. I was right behind her, and I
looked forbiddingly back at them so they would think she
was my wife.

We were lucky; we got a table to ourselves. Linda
shrugged off her cape and waved us toward the food. "Go
on," she said. She sat down and opened her purse. When I
looked back she was lighting a cigarette.

"You're pretty quiet tonight," Crosley said as we filled
our plates. "You pissed off about something?"

"Maybe I'm just quiet, Crosley, you know?"

He speared a slice of meat and said, "When she called
you El Negro, that didn't mean she thought you were a
Negro. She just said that because your hair is dark. Mine is
light, that's how come she called me El Blanco."

"I know that, Crosley. Jesus. You think I couldn't figure
that out? Give me some credit, okay?" Then, as we moved
around the table, I said, "You speak Spanish?"

"*Un poco.* Actually more like *un poquito.*"

"What's García mad about?"

"Money. Something about money."

"Like what?"

"That's all I could get. But it's definitely about money."

I'd meant to start off slow, but by the time I reached the end of the table my plate was full. Potato salad, ham, jumbo shrimp, toast, barbecued beef, eggs Benny. Crosley's was full too. We walked back toward Linda, who was leaning forward on her elbows and looking around the barn. She took a long drag off her cigarette, lifted her chin, and blew a stream of smoke up toward the rafters. I sat across from her. "Scoot down," Crosley said, and bumped in beside me.

She watched us eat for a while.

"So," she said, "El Blanco. Are you from New York?"

Crosley looked up in surprise. "No, ma'am," he said. "I'm from Virginia."

Linda stabbed out her cigarette. Her long fingernails were painted the same deep red as the lipstick smears on her cigarette butt. She said, "I just came from New York and I can tell you that is one crazy place. Just incredible. Listen to this. I am in a taxicab, you know, and we are stopping in this traffic jam for a long time and there is a taxicab next to us with this fellow in it who stares at me. Like this, you know." She made her eyes go round. "Of course I ignore him. So guess what, my door opens and he gets into my cab. 'Excuse me,' he says, 'I want to marry you.' 'That's nice,' I say. 'Ask my husband.' 'I don't care about your husband,' he says. 'I don't care about my wife, either.' Of course I had to laugh. 'Okay,' he says. 'You think that's funny? How about this.' Then he says—" Linda looked sharply at each of us. She sniffed and made a face. "He says things you would never believe. Never. He wants to do this and he wants to do that. Well, I act like I am about to scream. I open my mouth like this. 'Hey,' he says, 'okay, okay. Relax.' Then he gets out and goes back to his taxicab. We are still sitting there for a long time again, and you know what he is doing? He is reading the newspaper. With his hat on. Go ahead, eat," she said to us, and nodded toward the food.

A tall blonde girl was carving fresh slices of roast beef onto a platter. She was hale and bosomy—I could see the laces on her bodice straining. Her cheeks glowed. Her bare arms and shoulders were ruddy with exertion. Crosley raised his eyebrows at me. I raised mine back, though my heart wasn't in it. She was a Viking dream, pure gemütlichkeit, but I was drunk on García's stepmother and in that condition you don't want a glass of milk, you want more of what's making you stumble and fall.

Crosley and I filled our plates again and headed back.

"I'm always hungry," he said.

"I know what you mean," I told him.

Linda smoked another cigarette while we ate. She watched the other tables as if she was at a movie. I tried to eat with a little finesse and so did Crosley, dabbing his lips with a napkin between every bulging mouthful, but some of the people around us had completely slipped their moorings. They ducked their heads low to receive their food, and while they chewed it up they looked around suspiciously and circled their plates with their forearms. A big family to our left was the worst. There was something competitive and desperate about them; they seemed to be eating their way toward a condition where they would never have to eat again. You would have thought they were refugees from a great hunger, that outside these walls the land was afflicted with drought and barrenness. I felt a kind of desperation myself; I felt like I was growing emptier with every bite I took.

There was a din in the air, a steady roar like that of a waterfall.

Linda looked around with a pleased expression. Though she bore no likeness to anyone here, she seemed completely at home. She sent us back for another plate, then dessert and coffee, and while we were finishing up she asked El Blanco if he had a girlfriend.

"No, ma'am," Crosley said. "We broke up," he added, and his red face turned almost purple. It was clear that he was lying.

"You. How about you?"

I nodded.

"Ha!" she said. "El Negro is the one! So. What's her name?"

"Jane."

"Jaaane," Linda drawled. "Okay, let's hear about Jaaane."

"Jane," I said again.

Linda smiled.

I told her everything. I told her how my girlfriend and I had met and what she looked like and what our plans were—everything. I told her more than everything, because I gave certain coy but definite suggestions about the extremes to which our passion had already driven us. I meant to impress her with my potency, to enflame her, to wipe that smile off her face, but the more I told her the more wolfishly she smiled and the more her eyes laughed at me.

Laughing eyes—now there's a cliché my English master would have eaten me alive for. "How exactly did these eyes laugh?" he would have asked, looking up from my paper while my classmates snorted around me. "Did they titter, or did they merely chortle? Did they give a great guffaw? Did they, perhaps, *scream* with laughter?"

I am here to tell you that eyes can scream with laughter. Linda's did. As I played Big Hombre for her I could see exactly how complete my failure was. I could hear her saying *Okay, El Negro, go on, talk about your little gorlfren, but we know what you want, don't we? You want to suck on my tongue and slobber on my titties and bury your face in me. That's what you want.*

Crosley interrupted me. "Ma'am . . ." he said, and nodded toward the door. García was leaning there with his arms crossed and an expression of fury on his face. When she looked at him he turned and walked out the door.

Her eyes went flat. She sat there for a moment. She began to take a cigarette from her case, then put it back and stood up. "We go," she said.

García was waiting in the car, rigid and silent. He said nothing on the drive back. Linda swung her foot and stared out the window at the passing houses and bright, moonlit fields. Just before we reached the school García leaned forward and began speaking to her in a low voice. She listened impassively and didn't answer. He was still talking when the limousine stopped in front of the headmaster's house. The driver opened the door. García fixed his eyes on her. Still impassive, she took her pocketbook out of her purse. She opened it and looked inside. She meditated over the contents, then withdrew a bill and offered it to García. It was a hundred-dollar bill. "Boolshit!" he said, and sat back. With no change of expression she turned and held the bill out to me. I didn't know what else to do but take it. She got another one from her pocketbook and presented it to Crosley, who hesitated even less than I did. Then she gave us the same false smile she had greeted us with, and said, "Good night, it was a pleasure to meet you. Good night, good night," she said to García.

The three of us got out of the limousine. I went a few steps and then slowed down, and turned to look back.

"Keep walking!" Crosley hissed.

García yelled something in Spanish as the driver closed the door. I faced around again and walked with Crosley across the quad. As we approached our dorm he quickened his pace. "I don't believe it," he whispered. "A hundred bucks." When we were inside he stopped and shouted, "A hundred bucks! A hundred dollars!"

"Pipe down," someone called.

"All right, all right. Fuck you!" he added.

We went up the stairs to our floor, laughing and banging into each other. "Do you believe it?" he said.

I shook my head. We were standing outside my door.

"No, really now, listen." He put his hands on my shoulders and looked into my eyes. He said, "Do you fucking *believe* it?"

I told him I didn't.

"Well, neither do I. I don't fucking believe it."

There didn't seem to be much to say after that. I would have invited Crosley in, but to tell the truth I still thought of him as a thief. We laughed a few more times and said good night.

My room was cold. I took the bill out of my pocket and looked at it. It was new and stiff, the kind of bill you associate with kidnappings. The picture of Franklin was surprisingly lifelike. I looked at it for a while. A hundred dollars was a lot of money then. I had never had a hundred dollars before, not in one chunk like this. To be on the safe side I taped it to a page in *Profiles in Courage*—page 100, so I wouldn't forget where it was.

I had trouble getting to sleep. The food I had eaten sat like a stone in me, and I was miserable about the things I'd said. I understood that I had been a liar and a fool. I kept shifting under the covers, then I sat up and turned on my reading lamp. I picked up the new picture my girlfriend had sent me, and closed my eyes, and when I had some peace of mind I renewed my promises to her.

We broke up a month after I got home. Her parents were away one night, and we seized the opportunity to make love in their canopied bed. This was the fifth time we'd made love. She got up immediately afterward and started putting her clothes on. When I asked her what the problem was, she wouldn't answer me. I thought, Oh, Christ, what now. "Come on," I said. "What's wrong?"

She was tying her shoes. She looked up and said, "You don't love me."

It surprised me to hear this, not so much that she said it but because it was true. Before this moment I hadn't known it was true, but it was—I didn't love her.

For a long time afterward I told myself that I'd never really loved her, but this wasn't true.

We're supposed to smile at the passions of the young, and at what we recall of our own passions, as if they were no more than a series of sweet frauds we'd fooled ourselves with and then wised up to. Not only the passion of boys and girls for each other but the others, too—passion for justice, for doing right, for turning the world around. All these come in their time under our wintry smiles. Yet there was nothing foolish about what we felt. Nothing merely young. I just wasn't up to it. I let the light go out.

Sometime later I heard a soft knock at my door. I was still wide awake. "Yeah," I said.

Crosley stepped inside. He was wearing a blue dressing gown of some silky material that shimmered in the dim light of the hallway. He said, "Have you got any Tums or anything?"

"No. I wish I did."

"You too, huh?" He closed the door and sat on my roommate's bunk. "Do you feel as bad as I do?"

"How bad do you feel?"

"Like I'm dying. I think there was something wrong with the shrimp."

"Come on, Crosley. You ate everything but the barn."

"So did you."

"That's right. That's why I'm not complaining."

He moaned and rocked back and forth on the bed. I

could hear real pain in his voice. I sat up. "You okay, Crosley?"

"I guess," he said.

"You want me to call the nurse?"

"God," he said. "No, that's all right." He kept rocking. Then, in a carefully offhand way, he said, "Look, is it okay if I just stay here for a while?"

I almost said no, then I caught myself. "Sure," I told him. "Make yourself at home."

He must have heard my hesitation. "Forget it," he said bitterly. "Sorry I asked." But he made no move to go.

I felt confused, tender toward Crosley because he was in pain, repelled because of what I'd heard about him. But maybe what I'd heard about him wasn't true. I wanted to be fair, so I said, "Hey Crosley, do you mind if I ask you a question?"

"That depends."

He was watching me, his arms crossed over his stomach. In the moonlight his dressing gown was iridescent as oil.

"Is it true that you got caught stealing?"

"You prick," he said. He looked down at the floor.

I waited.

"You want to hear about it," he said, "just ask someone. Everybody knows all about it, right?"

"I don't."

"That's right, you don't. You don't know shit about it and neither does anyone else." He raised his head. "The really hilarious part is, I didn't actually get caught stealing it, I got caught putting it back. Not to make excuses. I stole it all right."

"Stole what?"

"The coat," he said. "Robinson's overcoat. Don't tell me you didn't know that."

"Well, I didn't."

"Then you must've been living in a cave or something. You know Robinson, right? Robinson was my roommate. He had this camel's hair overcoat, this really just beautiful overcoat. I kind of got obsessed with it. I thought about it all the time. Whenever he went somewhere without it, I'd put it on and stand in front of the mirror. Then one day I just took the fucker. I stuck it in my locker over at the gym. Robinson was really upset. He'd go to his closet ten, twenty times a day, like he thought the coat had just gone for a walk or something. So anyway, I brought it back. Robinson came into the room right when I was hanging it up." Crosley bent forward suddenly, then leaned back.

"You're lucky they didn't kick you out."

"I wish they had," he said. "The dean wanted to play Jesus. He got all choked up over the fact that I'd brought it back." Crosley rubbed his arms. "Man, did I want that coat. It was ridiculous how much I wanted that coat. You know?" He looked right at me. "Do you know what I'm talking about?"

I nodded.

"Really?"

"Yes."

"Good." Crosley lay back against the pillow, then lifted his feet onto the bed. "Say," he said, "I think I figured out how come García invited me."

"Yeah?"

"He was mad at his stepmother, right? He wanted to punish her."

"So?"

"So I'm the punishment. He probably heard I was the biggest douchebag in school, and figured whoever came with me would have to be a douchebag too. That's my theory, anyway."

I started laughing. It killed my stomach but I couldn't

stop. Crosley said, "Come on, man, don't make me laugh," and he started too, laughing and moaning at the same time.

We lay without talking, then Crosley said, "El Negro."

"Yeah."

"What are you going to do with your C-note?"

"I don't know. What are you going to do?"

"Buy a woman."

"Buy a woman?"

"I haven't gotten laid in a really long time. In fact," he said, "I've never gotten laid."

"Me either."

I thought about his words. *Buy a woman*. He could actually do it. I could do it myself. I didn't have to wait, didn't have to burn like this for month after month until Jane decided she was ready to give me relief. Three months was a long time to wait. It was an unreasonable time to wait for anything if you had no good reason to wait, if you could just buy what you needed. And to think that you could buy this—buy a mouth for your mouth, and arms and legs to wrap you tight. I had never considered this before. I thought of the money in my book. I could almost feel it there. Pure possibility.

Jane would never know. It wouldn't hurt her at all, and in a certain way it might help, because it was going to be very awkward at first if neither of us had any experience. As a man, I should know what I was doing. Everything would be a lot better that way.

I told Crosley that I liked his idea. "The time has come to lose our innocence," I said.

"*Exactamente*," he said.

And so we sat up and took counsel, leaning toward each other from the beds, holding our swollen bellies, whispering back and forth about how this thing might be done, and where, and when.

Lady's Dream

*L*ady's suffocating. Robert can't stand to have the windows down because the air blowing into the car bothers his eyes. The fan is on but only at the lowest speed, as the sound annoys him. Lady's head is getting heavy, and when she blinks she has to raise her eyelids by an effort of will. The heat and dampness of her skin give her the sensation of a fever. She's beginning to see things in the lengthening moments when her eyes are closed, things more distinct and familiar than the dipping wires and blur of trees and the silent staring man she sees when they're open.

"Lady?" Robert's voice calls her back, but she keeps her eyes closed.

That's him to the life. Can't stand her sleeping when he's not. He'd have some good reason to wake her, though. Never a mean motive. Never. When he's going to ask somebody for a favor he always calls first and just passes the time, then calls back the next day and says how great it was talking to them, he enjoyed it so much he forgot to ask if they'd mind doing something for him. Has no idea he does this. She's never heard him tell a lie, not even to make a story better. Tells the most boring stories. Just lethal. Considers every word. Considers everything. Early January he buys twelve vacuum cleaner bags and writes a different month on each one so she'll remember to change them. Of course she goes as long as she can on every bag and throws away the extras at the end of the year, because otherwise he'd find them and know. Not say anything—just know. Once she threw away seven. Sneaked them outside through the snow and stuffed them in the garbage can.

Considerate. Everything a matter of principle. Justice for all, yellow brown black or white they are precious in his sight. Can't say no to any charity but always forgets to send the money. Asks her questions about his own self. *Who's that actress I like so much? What's my favorite fish?* Is calm in every circumstance. Polishes his glasses all the time. They gleam so you can hardly see his eyes. Has to sleep on the right side of the bed. The sheets have to be white. Any other color gives him nightmares, forget about patterns. Patterns would kill him. Wears a hardhat when he works around the house. Says her name a hundred times a day. Always has. Any excuse.

He loves her name. Lady. Married her name. Shut her up in her name. Shut her up.

"Lady?"

Sorry, sir. Lady's gone.

She knows where she is. She's back home. Her father's away but her mother's home and her sister Jo. Lady hears their voices. She's in the kitchen running water into a glass, letting it overflow and pour down her fingers until it's good and cold. She lifts the glass and drinks her fill and sets the glass down, then walks slow as a cat across the kitchen and down the hall to the bright doorway that opens onto the porch where her mother and sister are sitting. Her mother straightens up and settles back again as Lady goes to the railing and leans on her elbows and looks down the street and then out to the fields beyond.

Lordalmighty it's hot.

Isn't it hot, though.

Jo is slouched in her chair, rolling a bottle of Coke on her forehead. I could just die.

Late again, Lady?

He'll be here.

Must have missed his bus again.

I suppose.

I bet those stupid cornpones were messing with him like they do, Jo says. I wouldn't be a soldier.

He'll be here. Else he'd call.

I wouldn't be a soldier.

Nobody asked you.

Now, girls.

I'd like to see you a soldier anyway, sleeping all day and laying in bed eating candy. Mooning around. Oh, General, don't make me march, that just wears me out. Oh, do I have to wear that old green thing, green just makes me look sick, haven't you got one of those in red? Why, I can't eat lima beans, don't you know about me and lima beans?

Now, Lady . . .

But her mother's laughing and so is Jo, in spite of herself. Oh, the goodness of that sound. And of her own voice. Just like singing. General, honey, you know I can't shoot that nasty thing, how about you ask one of those old boys to shoot it for me, they just love to shoot off their guns for Jo Kay.

Lady!

The three of them on the porch, waiting but not waiting. Sufficient unto themselves. Nobody has to come.

But Robert is on his way. He's leaning his head against the window of the bus and trying to catch his breath. He missed the first bus and had to run to catch this one because his sergeant found fault with him during inspection and stuck him on a cleanup detail. The sergeant hates his guts. He's an ignorant cracker and Robert is an educated man from Vermont, an engineer just out of college, quit Shell Oil in Louisiana to enlist the day North Korea crossed the parallel. The only Yankee in his company. Robert says when they get overseas there won't be any more Yankees and Southerners, just Americans. Lady likes him for believing that, but she gives him the needle because she knows it isn't true.

He changed uniforms in a hurry and didn't check the mirror before he left the barracks. There's a smudge on his right cheek. Shoe polish. His face is flushed and sweaty, his shirt soaked through. He's watching out the window and reciting a poem to himself. He's a great one for poems, this Robert. He has poems for running and poems for drill and poems for going to sleep, and poems for when the rednecks start getting him down.

> Out of the night that covers me,
> Black as the Pit from pole to pole,
> I thank whatever Gods may be
> For my unconquerable soul.

That's the poem he uses to fortify himself. He thinks it over and over even when they're yelling in his face. It keeps him strong. Lady laughs when he tells her things like this, and he always looks at her a little surprised and then he laughs too, to show he likes her sass, though he doesn't. He thinks it's just her being young and spoiled and that it'll go away if he can get her out of that house and away from her family and among sensible people who don't think everything's a joke. In time it'll wear off and leave her quiet and dignified and respectful of life's seriousness—leave her pure Lady.

That's what he thinks some days. Most days he sees no hope at all. He thinks of taking her home, into the house of his father, and when he imagines what she might say to his father he starts hearing his own excuses and apologies. Then he knows that it's impossible. Robert has picked up some psychology here and there, and he believes he understands how he got himself into this mess. It's rebellion. Subconscious, of course. A subconscious rebellion against his father, falling in love with a girl like Lady. Because you don't fall in love. No. Life isn't a song. You choose to fall in love. And there are reasons for that choice, just as there's a reason for every choice, if you get to the bottom of it. Once you figure out your reasons, you master your choices. It's as simple as that.

Robert is looking out the window without really seeing anything.

It's impossible. Lady is just a kid, she doesn't know anything about life. There's a rawness to her that will take years to correct. She's spoiled and willful and half-wild, except for her tongue, which is all wild. And she's Southern, not that there's anything wrong with that per se, but a particular kind of Southern. Not trash, as she would put it, but too proud of not being trash. Irrational. Superstitious. Clannish.

And what a clan it is, clan Cobb. Mr. Cobb a suspender-snapping paint salesman always on the road, full of drummer's banter and jokes about nigras and watermelon. Mrs. Cobb a morning-to-night gossip, weepily religious, content to live on her daughters' terms rather than raise them to woman's estate with discipline and right example. And the sister. Jo Kay. You can write that sad story before it happens.

All in all, Robert can't imagine a better family than the Cobbs to beat his father over the head with. That must be why he's chosen them, and why he has to undo that choice. He's made up his mind. He meant to tell her last time, but there was no chance. Today. No matter what. She won't understand. She'll cry. He will be gentle about it. He'll say she's a fine girl but too young. He'll say that it isn't fair to ask her to wait for him when who knows what might happen, and then to follow him to a place she's never been, far from family and friends.

He'll tell Lady anything but the truth, which is that he's ashamed to have picked her to use against his father. That's his own fight. He's been running from it for as long as he can remember, and he knows he has to stop. He has to face the man.

He will, too. He will, after he gets home from Korea. His father will have to listen to him then. Robert will make him listen. He will tell him, he will face his father and tell him . . .

Robert's throat tightens and he sits up straight. He hears himself breathing in quick shallow gasps and wonders if anyone else has noticed. His heart is kicking. His mouth is dry. He closes his eyes and forces himself to breathe more slowly and deeply, imitating calm until it becomes almost real.

They pass the power company and the Greyhound station. Red-faced soldiers in shiny shoes stand around out front smoking. The bus stops on a street lined with bars and the other men get off, hooting and pushing one another. There's just Robert and four women left on board. They turn off Jackson and bump across the railroad tracks and head east past the lumberyard. Black men are throwing planks into a truck, their shirts off, skin gleaming in the hazy light. Then they're gone behind a fence. Robert pulls the cord for his stop, waits behind a wide woman in a flowered dress. The flesh swings like hammocks under her arms. She takes forever going down the steps.

The sun dazzles his eyes. He pulls down the visor of his cap and walks to the corner and turns right. This is Arsenal Street. Lady lives two blocks down where the street runs into fields. There's no plan to the way it ends—it just gives out. From here on there's nothing but farms for miles. At night Lady and Jo Kay steal strawberries from the field behind their house, dish them up with thick fresh cream and grated chocolate. The strawberries have been stewing in the heat all day and burst open at the first pressure of the teeth. Robert disapproves of reaping another man's harvest, though he eats his share and then some. The season's about over. He'll be lucky if he gets any tonight.

He's thinking about strawberries when he sees Lady on the porch, and at that moment the sweetness of that taste fills his mouth. He stops as if he just remembered something, then comes toward her again. Her lips are moving but he can't hear her, he's aware of nothing but the taste in his mouth, and the closer he comes the stronger it gets. His pace quickens, his hand goes out for the railing. He takes the steps as if he means to devour her.

No, she's saying, no. She's talking to him and to the girl whose life he seeks. She knows what will befall her if she lets him have it. Stay here on this porch with your mother and your sister, they will soon have need of you. Gladden your father's eye yet awhile. This man is not for you. He will patiently school you half to death. He will kindly take you among unbending strangers to watch him fail to be brave. To suffer his carefulness, and to see your children writhe under it and fight it off with every kind of self-hurting recklessness. To be changed. To hear yourself, and not know who is speaking. Wait, young Lady. Bide your time.

"Lady?"

It's no good. The girl won't hear. Even now she's bending toward him as he comes up the steps. She reaches for his cheek, to brush away the smudge he doesn't know is there. He thinks it's something else that makes her do it, and his fine lean face confesses everything, asks everything. There's no turning back from this touch. She can't be stopped. She has a mind of her own, and she knows something Lady doesn't. She knows how to love him.

Lady hears her name again.

Wait, sir.

She blesses the girl. Then she turns to the far-rolling fields she used to dream an ocean, this house the ship that ruled it. She takes a last good look, and opens her eyes.

The Night in Question

*F*rances had come to her brother's apartment to hold his hand over a disappointment in love, but Frank ate his way through half the cherry pie she'd brought him and barely mentioned the woman. He was in an exalted state over a sermon he'd heard that afternoon. Dr. Violet had outdone himself, Frank said. This was his best; this was the gold standard. Frank wanted to repeat it to Frances, the way he used to act out movie scenes for her when they were young.

"Gotta run, Franky."

"It's not that long," Frank said. "Five minutes. Ten—at the outside."

Three years earlier he had driven Frances' car into a highway abutment and almost died, then almost died again, in detox, of a *grand mal* seizure. Now he wanted to preach sermons at her. She supposed she was grateful. She said she'd give him ten minutes.

It was a muggy night, but as always Frank wore a long-sleeved shirt to hide the weird tattoos he woke up with one morning when he was stationed in Manila. The shirt was white, starched and crisply ironed. The tie he'd worn to church was still cinched up hard under his prominent Adam's apple. A big man in a small room, he paced in front of the couch as he gathered himself to speak. He favored his left leg, whose knee had been shattered in the crash; every time his right foot came down, the dishes clinked in the cupboards.

"Okay, here goes," he said. "I'll have to fill in here and there, but I've got most of it." He continued to walk, slowly, deliberately, hands behind his back, head bent at an angle that suggested meditation. "My dear friends," he said, "you may have read in the paper not long ago of a man of our state, a parent like many of yourselves here today . . . but a parent with a terrible choice to make. His name is Mike Bolling. He's a railroad man, Mike, a switchman, been with the railroad ever since he finished high school, same as his father and grandfather before him. He and Janice've been married ten years now. They were hoping for a whole houseful of kids, but the Lord decided to give them one instead, a very special one. That was nine years ago. Benny, they named him—after Janice's father. He died when she was just a youngster, but she remembered his big lopsided grin and the way he threw back his head when he laughed, and she was hoping some of her dad's spirit would rub off on his name. Well, it turned out she got all the spirit she could handle, and then some.

"Benny. He came out in high gear and never shifted down. Mike liked to say you could run a train off him, the energy he had. Good student, natural athlete, but his big thing was mechanics. One of those boys, you put him in the same room with a clock and he's got it in pieces before you can turn around. By the time he was in second grade he could put the clocks back together, not to mention the vacuum cleaner and the TV and the engine of Mike's old lawn mower."

This didn't sound like Frank. Frank was plain in his

speech, neither formal nor folksy, so spare and sometimes harsh that his jokes sounded like challenges, or insults. Frances was about the only one who got them. This tone was putting her on edge. Something terrible was going to happen in the story, something Frances would regret having heard. She knew that. But she didn't stop him. Frank was her little brother, and she would deny him nothing.

When Frank was still a baby, not even walking yet, Frank Senior, their father, had set out to teach his son the meaning of the word no. At dinner he'd dangle his wristwatch before Frank's eyes, then say *no!* and jerk it back just as Frank grabbed for it. When Frank persisted, Frank Senior would slap his hand until he was howling with fury and desire. This happened night after night. Frank would not take the lesson to heart; as soon as the watch was offered, he snatched at it. Frances followed her mother's example and said nothing. She was eight years old, and while she feared her father's attention she also missed it, and resented Frank's obstinacy and the disturbance it caused. Why couldn't he learn? Then her father slapped Frank's face. This was on New Year's Eve. Frances still remembered the stupid tasseled hats they were all wearing when her father slapped her baby brother. In the void of time after the slap there was no sound but the long rush of air into Frank's lungs as, red-faced, twisting in his chair, he gathered himself to scream. Frank Senior lowered his head. Frances saw that he'd surprised himself and was afraid of what would follow. She looked at her mother, whose eyes were closed. In later years Frances tried to think of a moment when their lives might have turned by even a degree, turned and gone some other way, and she always came back to this instant when her father knew the wrong he had done, was shaken and open to rebuke. What might have happened if her mother had come flying out of her chair and stood over him and told him to stop, now and forever?

Or if she had only *looked* at him, confirming his shame? But her eyes were closed, and stayed closed until Frank blasted them with his despair and Frank Senior left the room. As Frances knew even then, her mother could not allow herself to see what she had no strength to oppose. Her heart was bad. Three years later she reached for a bottle of ammonia, said "Oh," sat down on the floor and died.

Frances did oppose her father. In defiance of his orders, she brought food to Frank's room when he was banished, stood up for him and told him he was right to stand up for himself. Frank Senior had decided that his son needed to be broken, and Frank would not break. He went after everything his father said no to, with Frances egging him on and mothering him when he got caught. In time their father ceased to give reasons for his displeasure. As his silence grew heavier, so did his hand. One night Frances grabbed her father's belt as he started after Frank, and when he flung her aside Frank head-rammed him in the stomach. Frances jumped on her father's back and the three of them crashed around the room. When it was over Frances was flat on the floor with a split lip and a ringing sound in her ears, laughing like a madwoman. Frank was crying. That was the first time.

Frank Senior said no to his son in everything, and Frances would say no to him in nothing. Frank was aware of her reluctance and learned to exploit it, most shamelessly in the months before his accident. He'd invaded her home, caused her trouble at work, nearly destroyed her marriage. To this day her husband had not forgiven Frances for what he called her complicity in that nightmare. But her husband had never been thrown across a room, or kicked, or slammed headfirst into a door. No one had ever spoken to him as her father had spoken to Frank. He did not understand what it was to be helpless and alone. No one should be alone in this world. Everyone should have someone who kept faith, no matter what, all the way.

"On the night in question," Frank said, "Mike's foreman called up and asked him to take another fellow's shift at the drawbridge station where he'd been working. A Monday night it was, mid-January, bitter cold. Janice was at a PTA meeting when Mike got the call, so he had no choice but to bring Benny along with him. It was against the rules, strictly speaking, but he needed the overtime and he'd done it before, more than once. Nobody ever said anything. Benny always behaved himself, and it was a good chance for him and Mike to buddy up, batch it a little. They'd talk and kid around, heat up some franks, then Mike would set Benny up with a sleeping bag and air mattress. A regular adventure.

"A bitter night, like I said. There was a furnace at the station, but it wasn't working. The guy Mike relieved had on his parka and a pair of mittens. Mike ribbed him about it, but pretty soon he and Benny put their own hats and gloves back on. Mike brewed up some hot chocolate, and they played gin rummy, or tried to—it's not that easy with gloves on. But they weren't thinking about winning or losing. It was good enough just being together, the two of them, with the cold wind blowing up against the windows. Father and son: what could be better than that? Then Mike had to raise the bridge for a couple of boats, and things got pretty tense because one of them steered too close to the bank and almost ran aground. The skipper had to reverse engines and go back downriver and take another turn at it. The whole business went on a lot longer than it should have, and by the time the second boat got clear Mike was running way behind schedule and under pressure to get the bridge down for the express train out of Portland. That was when he noticed Benny was missing."

Frank stopped by the window and looked out in an unseeing way. He seemed to be contemplating whether to go on. But then he turned away from the window and started in again, and Frances understood that this little moment of reflection was just another part of the sermon.

"Mike calls Benny's name. No answer. He calls him again, and he doesn't spare the volume. You have to understand the position Mike is in. He has to get the bridge down for that train and he's got just about enough time to do it. He doesn't know where Benny is, but he has a pretty good idea. Just where he isn't supposed to be. Down below, in the engine room.

"The engine room. The mill, as Mike and the other operators call it. You can imagine the kind of power that's needed to raise and lower a drawbridge, aside from the engine itself—all the winches and levers, pulleys and axles and wheels and so on. Massive machinery. Gigantic screws turning everywhere, gears with teeth like file cabinets. They've got catwalks and little crawlways through the works for the mechanics, but nobody goes down there unless they know what they're doing. You have to know what you're doing. You have to know exactly where to put your feet, and you've got to keep your hands in close and wear all the right clothes. And even if you know what you're doing, you never go down there when the bridge is being moved. Never. There's just too much going on, too many ways of getting snagged and pulled into the works. Mike has told Benny a hundred times, stay out of the mill. That's the iron rule when Benny comes out to the station. But Mike made the mistake of taking him down for a quick look one day when the engine was being serviced, and he saw how Benny lit up at the sight of all that steel, all that machinery. Benny was just dying to get his hands on those wheels and gears, see how everything fit together. Mike could feel it pulling at Benny like a big magnet. He always kept a close eye on him after that, until this one night, when he got distracted. And now Benny's down in there. Mike knows it as sure as he knows his own name."

Frances said, "I don't want to hear this story."

Frank gave no sign that he'd heard her. She was going to say something else, but made a sour face and let him go on.

"To get to the engine room, Mike would have to go through the passageway to the back of the station and either wait for the elevator or climb down the emergency ladder. He doesn't have time to do the one or the other. He doesn't have time for anything but lowering the bridge, and just barely enough time for that. He's got to get that bridge down now or the train is going into the river with everyone on board. This is the position he's in; this is the choice he has to make. His son, his Benjamin, or the people on that train.

"Now, let's take a minute to think about the people on that train. Mike's never met any of them, but he's lived long enough to know what they're like. They're like the rest of us. There are some who know the Lord, and love their neighbors, and live in the light. And there are the others. On this train are men who whisper over cunning papers and take from the widow even her mean portion. On this train is the man whose factories kill and maim his workers. There are thieves on this train, and liars, and hypocrites. There is the man whose wife is not enough for him, who cannot be happy until he possesses every woman who walks the earth. There is the false witness. There is the bribe-taker. There is the woman who abandons her husband and children for her own pleasure. There is the seller of spoiled goods, the coward, and the usurer, and there is the man who lives for his drug, who will do anything for that false promise—steal from those who give him work, from his friends, his family, yes, even from his own family, scheming for their pity, borrowing in bad faith, breaking into their very homes. All these are on the train, awake and hungry as wolves, and also on the train are the sleepers, the sleepers with open eyes who sleepwalk through their days, neither doing evil nor resisting it, like soldiers who lie down as if dead and will not join the battle, not for their cities and homes, not even for their wives and children. For such people, how can Mike give up his son, his Benjamin, who is guilty of nothing?

"He can't. Of course he can't, not on his own. But Mike isn't on his own. He knows what we all know, even when we try to forget it: we are never alone, ever. We are in our Father's presence in the light of day and in the dark of night, even in that darkness where we run from Him, hiding our faces like fearful children. He will not leave us. No. He will never leave us alone. Though we lock every window and bar every door, still He will enter. Though we empty our hearts and turn them to stone, yet shall He make His home there.

"He will not leave us alone. He is with all of you, as He is with me. He is with Mike, and also with the bribe-taker on the train, and the woman who needs her friend's husband, and the man who needs a drink. He knows their needs better than they do. He knows that what they truly need is Him, and though they flee His voice He never stops telling them that He is there. And at this moment, when Mike has nowhere to hide and nothing left to tell himself, then he can hear, and he knows that he is not alone, and he knows what it is that he must do. It has been done before, even by Him who speaks, the Father of All, who gave His own son, His beloved, that others might be saved."

"No!" Frances said.

Frank stopped and looked at Frances as if he couldn't remember who she was.

"That's it," she said. "That's my quota of holiness for the year."

"But there's more."

"I know, I can see it coming. The guy kills his kid, right? I have to tell you, Frank, that's a crummy story. What're we supposed to get from a story like that—we should kill our own kid to save some stranger?"

"There's more to it than that."

"Okay, then, make it a trainload of strangers, make it *ten* trainloads of strangers. I should do this because the so-called Father of All did it? Is that the point? How do people think up stuff like this, anyway? It's an awful story."

"It's true."

"*True?* Franky. Please, you're not a moron."

"Dr. Violet knows a man who was on that train."

"I'll just bet he does. Let me guess." Frances screwed her eyes shut, then popped them open. "The drug addict! Yes, and he reformed afterward and worked with street kids in Brazil and showed everybody that Mike's sacrifice was not in vain. Is that how it goes?"

"You're missing the point, Frances. It isn't about that. Let me finish."

"No. It's a terrible story, Frank. People don't act like that. I sure as hell wouldn't."

"You haven't been asked. He doesn't ask us to do what we can't do."

"I don't care what He asks. Where'd you learn to talk like that, anyway? You don't even sound like yourself."

"I had to change. I had to change the way I thought about things. Maybe I sound a little different too."

"Yeah, well you sounded better when you were drunk."

Frank seemed about to say something, but didn't. He

backed up a step and lowered himself into a hideous plaid La-Z-Boy left behind by the previous tenant. It was stuck in the upright position.

"I don't care if the Almighty poked a gun in my ear, I would never do that," Frances said. "Not in a million years. Neither would you. Honest, now, little brother, would you grind me up if I was the one down in the mill, would you push the Francesburger button?"

"It isn't a choice I have to make."

"Yeah, yeah, I know. But say you did."

"I don't. He doesn't hold guns to our heads."

"Oh, really? What about hell, huh? What do you call that? But so what. Screw hell, I don't care about hell. Do I get crunched or not?"

"Don't put me to the test, Frances. It's not your place."

"I'm down in the mill, Frank. I'm stuck in the gears and here comes the train with Mother Teresa and five hundred sinners on board, *whoo whoo, whoo whoo*. Who, Frank, who? Who's it going to be?"

Frances wanted to laugh. Glumly erect in the chair, hands gripping the armrests, Frank looked like he was about to take off into a hurricane. But she kept that little reflection to herself. Frank was thinking, and she had to let him. She knew what his answer would be—in the end there could be no other answer—but he couldn't just say *she's my sister* and let it go at that. No, he'd have to noodle up some righteous, high-sounding reasons for choosing her. And maybe he wouldn't, at first, maybe he'd chicken out and come up with the Bible-school answer. Frances was ready for that, she was up for a fight; she could bring him around. Frances didn't mind a fight, and she especially didn't mind fighting for her brother. For her brother she'd fought neighborhood punks, snotty teachers and unappreciative coaches, loan sharks, landlords, bouncers. From the time she was a scabby-kneed girl she'd taken on her own father, and if push came to shove she'd take on the Father of All, that incomprehensible bully. She was ready. It would be like old times, the two of them waiting in her room upstairs while Frank Senior worked himself into a rage below, muttering, slamming doors, stinking up the house with the cigars he puffed when he was on a tear. She remembered it all—the tremor in her legs, the hammering pulse in her neck as the smell of smoke grew stronger. She could still taste that smoke and hear her father's steps on the stairs, Frank panting beside her, moving closer, his voice whispering her name and her own voice answering as fear gave way to ferocity and unaccountable joy, *It's okay, Franky. I'm here.*

Firelight

My mother swore we'd never live in a boarding-house again, but circumstances did not allow her to keep this promise. She decided to change cities; we had to sleep somewhere. This boardinghouse was worse than the last, unfriendly, funereal, heavy with the smells that disheartened people allow themselves to cultivate. On the floor below ours a retired merchant seaman was coughing his lungs out. He was a friendly old guy, always ready with a compliment for my mother as we climbed past the dim room where he sat smoking on the edge of his bed. During the day we felt sorry for him, but at night, as we lay in wait for the next racking seizure, feeling the silence swell with it, we hated him. I did, anyway.

My mother said this was only temporary. We were definitely getting out of there. To show me and maybe herself that she meant business, she went through the paper during breakfast every Saturday morning and circled the advertisements for furnished apartments that sounded, as she put it, "right for our needs." I liked that expression. It made me feel as if our needs had some weight in the world, and would have to be reckoned with. Then, putting on her shrewd face, my mother compared the rents and culled out the most expensive apartments and also the very cheap ones. We knew the story on those, the dinky fridge and weeping walls, the tub sinking through the bathroom floor, the wife-beater upstairs. We'd been that route. When my mother had five or six possibilities, she called to make sure they were still open and we spent the day going from one to another.

We couldn't actually take a place yet. The landlords wanted first and last months' rent, plus cleaning deposit, and it was going to be a while before my mother could put all that together. I understood this, but every Saturday my mother repeated it again so I wouldn't get carried away. We were just looking. Getting a feel for the market.

There is pleasure to be found in the purchase of goods and services. I enjoy it myself now, playing the part of a man who knows what he wants and can take it home with him. But in those days I was mostly happy just to look at things. And that was lucky for me, because we did a power of looking, and no buying.

My mother wasn't one of those comparison shoppers who head straight for the price tag, shaking their faces and beefing about the markup to everyone in sight. She had no great interest in price. She had no money, either, but it went deeper than that. She liked to shop because she felt at home in stores and was interested in the merchandise. Sales clerks waited on her without impatience, seeing there was nothing mean or trivial in her curiosity, this curiosity that kept her so young and drove her so hard. She just had to see what was out there.

We'd always shopped, but that first fall in Seattle, when we were more broke than we'd ever been, we really hit our stride. We looked at leather luggage. We looked at televi-

sions in large Mediterranean consoles. We looked at an-
tiques and Oriental rugs. Looking at Oriental rugs isn't
something you do lightly, because the men who sell them
have to work like dogs, dragging them down from these
tall teetering piles and then humping them over to you,
sweating and gasping, staggering under the weight, their
faces woolly with lint. They tend to be small men. You can't
be squeamish. You have to be free of shame, absolutely sure
of your right to look at what you cannot buy. And so we
were.

When the new fashions came in, my mother tried them
on while I watched. She had once been a model and knew
how to strike attitudes before the mirror, how to walk casually away and then stop, canting one hip and glancing over
her shoulder as if someone had just called her name. When
she turned to me I expressed my judgments with a smile, a
shrug, a sour little shake of the head. I thought she was
beautiful in everything but I felt obliged to discriminate.
She didn't like too much admiration. It suffocated her.

We looked at copper cookware. We looked at lawn furniture and pecan dining room sets. We spent one whole
day at a marina, studying the inventory of a bankrupt
Chris-Craft dealership. *The Big Giveaway*, they called it. It
was the only sale we ever made a point of going to.

My mother wore a smart gray suit when we went house
hunting. I wore my little gentleman's outfit, a V-neck
sweater with a bow tie. The sweater had the words *Fraternity Row* woven across the front. We looked respectable, as,
on the whole, we were. We also looked solvent.

On this particular day we were touring apartments in
the university district. The first three we looked at were decent enough, but the fourth was a wreck—the last tenant, a
woman, must have lived there like an animal in a cave.

Someone had tried to clean it up but the job was hopeless. The place smelled like rotten meat, even with the windows open and the cold air blowing through. Everything felt sticky. The landlord said that the woman had been depressed over the breakup of her marriage. Though he talked about a paint job and new carpets, he seemed discouraged and soon fell silent. The three of us walked through the rooms, then back outside. The landlord could tell we weren't biting. He didn't even offer us a card.

We had one more apartment to look at, but my mother said she'd seen enough. She asked me if I wanted to go down to the wharf, or home, or what. Her mouth was set, her face drawn. She tried to sound agreeable but she was in a black mood. I didn't like the idea of going back to the house, back to the room, so I said why didn't we walk up to the university and take a look around.

She squinted up the street. I thought she was going to say no. "Sure," she said. "Why not? As long as we're here."

We started walking. There were big maples along the sidewalk. Fallen leaves scraped and eddied around our legs as the breeze gusted.

"You don't *ever* let yourself go like that," my mother said, hugging herself and looking down. "There's no excuse for it."

She sounded mortally offended. I knew I hadn't done anything, so I kept quiet. She said, "I don't care what happens, there is no excuse to give up like that. Do you hear what I'm saying?"

"Yes, ma'am."

A group of Chinese came up behind us, ten or twelve of them, all young men, talking excitedly. They parted around us, still talking, and rejoined like water flowing around a stone. We followed them up the street and across the road to the university, where we wandered among the buildings as the light began to fail and the wind turned raw. This was the first really cold day since we'd moved here and I wasn't dressed for it. But I said nothing, because I still didn't want to go home. I had never set foot on a campus before and was greedily measuring it against my idea of what it should look like. It had everything. Old-looking buildings with stone archways and high, arched windows. Rich greenswards. Ivy. The leaves of the ivy had turned red. High on the west-facing walls, in what was left of the sunshine, the red leaves glittered as the wind stirred them. Every so often a great roar went up from Husky Stadium, where a game was in progress. Each time I heard it I felt a thrill of complicity and belonging. I believed that I was in place here, and that the students we passed on the brick walkways would look at me and see one of themselves—*Fraternity Row*—if it weren't for the woman beside me, her hand on my shoulder. I began to feel the weight of that hand.

My mother didn't notice. She was in good spirits again, flushed with the cold and with memories of days like this at Yale and Trinity, when she used to get free tickets to football games from a girlfriend who dated a player. She had dated one of the players herself, an All-American quarterback from Yale named Dutch Diefenbacker. He'd wanted to marry her, she added carelessly.

"You mean he actually asked you?"

"He gave me a ring. My father sold it to him. He'd bought it for this woman he had a crush on, but she wouldn't accept it. What she actually said was 'Why, I wouldn't marry an old man like you!'" My mother laughed.

"Wait a minute," I said. "You had a chance to marry an All-American from Yale?"

"Sure."

"So why didn't you?"

We stopped beside a fountain clotted with leaves. My mother stared into the water. "I don't know. I was pretty young then, and Dutch wasn't what you'd call a scintillating guy. He was nice . . . just dull. Very dull." She drew a deep breath and said, with some violence, "God, he was boring!"

"I would've married him," I said. I'd never heard about this before. That my mother, out of schoolgirl snobbery, had deprived me of an All-American father from Yale was outrageous. I would be rich now, and have a collie. Everything would be different.

We circled the fountain and headed back the way we'd come. When we reached the road my mother asked me if I wanted to look at the apartment we'd skipped. "Oh, what the heck," she said, seeing me hesitate. "It's around here somewhere. We might as well make a clean sweep."

I was cold, but because I hadn't said anything so far I thought it would sound false if I complained now, false and babyish. She stopped two girls wearing letter sweaters—co-eds, I thought, finding a cheap, keen excitement in the word—and while they gave her directions I studied the display in a bookstore window, as if I just happened to be standing beside this person who didn't know her way around.

The evening was clear and brief. At a certain moment the light flared weakly, and then it was gone. We walked several blocks, into a neighborhood of Victorian houses whose windows, seen from the empty street, glowed with rich, exclusive light. The wind blew at our backs. I was starting to shake. I still didn't tell my mother. I knew I should have said something earlier, that I'd been stupid not to, and now I fastened all my will on the effort to conceal this stupidity by maintaining it.

We stopped in front of a house with a turret. The upper story was dark. "We're late," I said.

"Not that late," my mother said. "Besides, the apartment's on the ground floor."

She walked up to the porch while I waited on the side-walk. I heard the muted chime of bells, and watched the windows for movement.

"Nuts . . . I should've called," my mother said. She'd just turned away when one of the two doors swung open and a man leaned out, a big man silhouetted in the bright doorway. "Yes?" he said. He sounded impatient, but when my mother turned to face him he added, more gently, "What can I do for you?" His voice was so deep I could al-most feel it, like coal rumbling down a chute.

She told him we were here about the apartment. "I guess we're a little late," she said.

"An hour late," he said.

My mother exclaimed surprise, said we'd been walking around the university and completely lost track of time. She was very apologetic but made no move to go, and it must have been clear to him that she had no intention of going until she'd seen the apartment. It was clear enough to me. I went down the walkway and up the porch steps.

He was big in every direction—tall and rotund with a massive head, a trophy head. He had the kind of size that provokes, almost inevitably, the nickname "Tiny," though I'm sure nobody ever called him that. He was too solemn, preoccupied, like a buffalo in the broadness and gravity of his face. He looked down at us through black-framed glasses. "Well, you're here," he said, not unkindly, and we followed him inside.

The first thing I saw was the fire. I was aware of other things, furniture, the church-like expanse of the room, but my eyes went straight to the flames. They burned with a hissing sound in a fireplace I could have walked into with-out stooping, or just about. A girl lay on her stomach in front of the fire, one bare foot raised and slowly twisting, her chin propped in her hand. She was reading a book. She went on reading it for a few moments after we came in, then sat up and said, very precisely, "Good evening." She had boobs. I could see them pushing at the front of her blouse. But she wasn't pretty. She was owlish and large and wore the same kind of glasses as the man, whom she closely and unfortunately resembled. She blinked constantly. I felt immediately at ease with her. I smiled and said "Hi," instead of assuming the indifference, even hostility, with which I treated pretty girls.

Something was in the oven, something chocolate. I went over to the fire and stood with my back to it, flexing my hands behind me.

"Oh yes, it's quite comfortable," the man said in answer to a comment of my mother's. He peered around curiously as if surprised to find himself here. The room was big, the biggest I'd ever seen in an apartment. We could never afford to live here, but I was already losing my grip on that fact.

"I'll go get my wife," the man said, then stayed where he was, watching my mother.

She was turning slowly, nodding to herself in a pensive way. "All this room," she said. "It makes you feel so free. How can you bear to give it up?"

At first he didn't answer. The girl started picking at something on the rug. Then he said, "We're ready for a bit of a change. Aren't we, Sister?"

She nodded without looking up.

A woman came in from the next room, carrying a plate of brownies. She was tall and thin. Deep furrows ran down her cheeks, framing her mouth like parentheses. Her gray hair was pulled into a ponytail. She moved toward us with slow, measured steps, as if carrying gifts to the altar, and set the plate on the coffee table. "You're just in time to have some of Dr. Avery's brownies," she said.

I thought she was referring to a recipe. Then the man hurried over and scooped up a handful, and I understood.

I understood not only that he was Dr. Avery, but also that the brownies belonged to him; his descent on the plate bore all the signs of jealous ownership. I was nervous about taking one, but Sister did it and survived, and even went back for another. I had a couple myself. As we ate, the woman slipped her arm behind Dr. Avery's back and leaned against him. The little I'd seen of marriage had disposed me to view public affection between husbands and wives as pure stagecraft—*Look, this is a home where people hug each other*—but she was so plainly happy to be where she was that I couldn't help feeling happy with her.

My mother prowled the room restlessly. "Do you mind if I look around?" she said.

Mrs. Avery asked Sister to show us the rest of the apartment.

More big rooms. Two of them had fireplaces. Above the mantel in the master bedroom hung a large photograph of a man with dark, thoughtful eyes. When I asked Sister who it was, she said, a shade importantly, "Gurdjieff."

I didn't mind her condescension. She was older, and bigger, and I suspected smarter than me. Condescension seemed perfectly in order.

"Gurdjieff," my mother said. "I've heard of him."

"*Gurdjieff*," Sister repeated, as though she'd said it wrong.

We went back to the living room and sat around the fire, Dr. and Mrs. Avery on the couch, my mother in a rocking chair across from them. Sister and I stretched out on the floor. She opened her book, and a moment later her foot rose into the air again and began its slow twisting motion. My mother and Mrs. Avery were talking about the apartment. I stared into the flames, the voices above me pleasant and meaningless until I heard my name mentioned. My mother was telling Mrs. Avery about our walk around the university. She said it was a beautiful campus.

"Beautiful?" Dr. Avery said. "What do you mean by beautiful?"

My mother looked at him. She didn't answer.

"I assume you're referring to the buildings."

"Sure. The buildings, the grounds. The general layout."

"Pseudo-Gothic humbug," Dr. Avery said. "A movie set."

"Dr. Avery believes that the university pays too much attention to appearances," Mrs. Avery said.

"That's all they pay attention to," Dr. Avery said.

"I wouldn't know about that," my mother said. "I'm not an expert on architecture. It looked nice enough to me."

"Yes, well that's the whole point, isn't it?" Dr. Avery said. "It *looks* like a university. The same with the so-called education they're selling. It's a counterfeit experience from top to bottom. Utterly hollow. All *materia*, no *anima*."

He lost me there, and I went back to looking at the flames. Dr. Avery rumbled on. He had been quiet before, but once he got started he didn't stop, and I wouldn't have wanted him to. The sound of his voice made me drowsy with assurance, like the drone of a car engine when you're lying on the backseat, going home from a long trip. Now and then Mrs. Avery spoke up, expressing concord with something the Doctor had said, making her complete agreement known; then he resumed. Sister shifted beside me. She yawned, turned a page. The logs settled in the fireplace, very softly, like some old sleeping dog adjusting his bones.

Dr. Avery talked for quite a while. Then my mother spoke my name. Nothing more, only my name. Dr. Avery went on as if he hadn't heard. He was leaning forward, one finger wagging to the cadence of his words, glasses glinting as his great head shook. I looked at my mother. She sat stiffly in the rocker, her hands kneading the purse in her lap. Her face was bleak, frozen. It was the expression she wore when she got trapped by some diehard salesman or a pair of Mormons who wouldn't go away. She wanted to leave.

I did not want to leave. Nodding by the fire, torpid and content, I had forgotten that this was not my home. The heat and the firelight worked on me like Dr. Avery's voice, lulling me into a state of familial serenity such as these people seemed to enjoy. I even managed to forget they were not my family, and that they too would soon be moving on. I made them part of my story without any sense that they had their own to live out.

What that was, I don't know. We never saw them again. But now, so many years later, I can venture a guess. My guess is that Dr. Avery had been denied tenure by the university, and that this wasn't the first to prove itself unequal to him, nor the last. I see him carrying his fight against mere appearances from one unworthy institution to the next, each of them refusing, with increasing vehemence, his call to spiritual greatness. Dr. Avery's colleagues, small minds joined to small hearts, ridicule him as a nuisance and a bore. His high-mindedness, they imply, is a cover for lack of distinction in his field, whatever that may be. Again and again they send him packing. Mrs. Avery consoles his wounded *anima* with unfailing loyalty, and ministers to his swelling *materia* with larger and larger batches of brownies. She believes in him. Her faith, whatever its foundation, is heroic. Not once does she imagine, as a lesser woman might, that her chances for common happiness — old friends, a place of her own, a life rooted in community— have been sacrificed not to some higher truth but to vanity and arrogance.

No, that part belongs to Sister. Sister will be the heretic. She has no choice, being their child. In time, not many years after this night, she will decide that the disappointments of her life can be traced to their failings. Who knows those failings better than Sister? There are scenes. Dr. Avery is accused of being himself, Mrs. Avery of being herself. The visits home from Barnard or Reed or wherever Sister's scholarship takes her, and then from the distant city where she works, become theatrical productions. Angry whispers in the kitchen, shouts at the dinner table, early departure. This goes on for years, but not forever. Sister makes peace with her parents. She even comes to cherish what she has resented, their refusal to talk and act as others do, their endless moving on, the bright splash of their oddity in the muddy flow. She finds she has no choice but to love them, and who can love them better than Sister?

It might have gone this way, or another way. I have made these people part of my story without knowing anything of theirs, just as I did that night, dreaming myself one of them. We were strangers. I'd spent maybe forty-five minutes in their apartment, just long enough to get warm and lose sight of the facts.

My mother spoke my name again. I stayed where I was. Usually I would have gotten to my feet without being prodded, not out of obedience but because it pleased me to anticipate her, to show off our teamwork. This time I just stared at her sullenly. She looked wrong in the rocking chair; she was too glamorous for it. I could see her glamor almost as a thing apart, another presence, a brassy impatient friend just dying to get her out of here, away from all this domesticity.

She said we ought to think about getting home. Sister raised her head and looked at me. I still didn't move. I could see my mother's surprise. She waited for me to do something, and when I didn't she rocked forward slowly and stood up. Everyone stood with her except me. I felt foolish and bratty sitting on the floor all by myself, but I stayed there anyway while she made the final pleasantries. When she moved toward the door, I got up and mumbled my good-byes, then followed her outside.

Dr. Avery held the door for us.

"I still think it's a pretty campus," my mother said.

He laughed—*Ho ho ho.* "Well, so be it," he said. "To each his own." He waited until we reached the sidewalk, then turned the light off and closed the door. It made a solid bang behind us.

"What was all that about?" my mother said.

I didn't answer.

"Are you feeling okay?"

"Yes." Then I said, "I'm a little cold."

"Cold? Why didn't you say something?" She tried to look concerned but I could see that she was glad to have a simple answer for what had happened back in the house.

She took off her suit jacket. "Here."

"That's okay."

"Put it on."

"Really, Mom. I'll be okay."

"Put it on, dimwit!"

I pulled the coat over my shoulders. We walked for a while. "I look ridiculous," I said.

"So . . . who cares?"

"I do."

"Okay, you do. *Sorry.* Boy, you're a regular barrel of laughs tonight."

"I'm not wearing this thing on the bus."

"Nobody said you had to wear it on the bus. You want to grab something to eat before we head back?"

I told her sure, fine, whatever she wanted.

"Maybe we can find a pizza place. Think you could eat some pizza?"

I said I thought I could.

A black dog with gleaming eyes crossed the street in our direction.

"Hello, sport," my mother said.

The dog trotted along beside us for a while, then took off.

I turned up the jacket collar and hunched my shoulders. "Are you still cold?"

"A little." I was shivering like crazy. It seemed to me I'd never been so cold, and I blamed my mother for it, for taking me outside again, away from the fire. I knew it wasn't her fault but I blamed her anyway—for this and the wind in my face and for every nameless thing that was not as it should be.

"Come here." She pulled me over and began to rub her hand up and down my arm. When I leaned away she held on and kept rubbing. It felt good. I wasn't really warm, but I was as warm as I was going to get.

"Just out of curiosity," my mother said, "what did you think of the campus? Honestly."

"I liked it."

"I thought it was great," she said.

"So did I."

"That big blowhard," she said. "Where does he get off?"

I have my own fireplace now. Where we live the winters are long and cold. The wind blows the snow sideways, the house creaks, the windows glaze over with ferns of ice. After dinner I lay the fire, building four walls of logs like a roofless cabin. That's the best way. Only greenhorns use the teepee method. My children wait behind me, jockeying for position, furiously arguing their right to apply the match. I tell them to do it together. Their hands shake with eagerness as they strike the matches and hold them to the crumpled paper, torching as many spots as they can before the kindling starts to crackle. Then they sit back on their heels and watch the flame engulf the cabin walls. Their faces are reverent.

My wife comes in and praises the fire, knowing the pride it gives me. She lies on the couch with her book but doesn't read it. I don't read mine, either. I watch the fire, watch the changing light on the faces of my family. I try to feel at home, and I do, almost entirely. This is the moment I dream of when I am far away; this is my dream of home. But in the very heart of it I catch myself bracing a little, as if in fear of being tricked. As if to really believe in it will somehow make it vanish, like a voice waking me from sleep.

Bullet in the Brain

*A*nders couldn't get to the bank until just before it closed, so of course the line was endless and he got stuck behind two women whose loud, stupid conversation put him in a murderous temper. He was never in the best of tempers anyway, Anders—a book critic known for the weary, elegant savagery with which he dispatched almost everything he reviewed.

With the line still doubled around the rope, one of the tellers stuck a "POSITION CLOSED" sign in her window and walked to the back of the bank, where she leaned against a desk and began to pass the time with a man shuffling papers. The women in front of Anders broke off their conversation and watched the teller with hatred. "Oh, that's nice," one of them said. She turned to Anders and added, confident of his accord, "One of those little human touches that keep us coming back for more."

Anders had conceived his own towering hatred of the teller, but he immediately turned it on the presumptuous crybaby in front of him. "Damned unfair," he said. "Tragic, really. If they're not chopping off the wrong leg, or bombing your ancestral village, they're closing their positions."

She stood her ground. "I didn't say it was tragic," she said. "I just think it's a pretty lousy way to treat your customers."

"Unforgivable," Anders said. "Heaven will take note."

She sucked in her cheeks but stared past him and said nothing. Anders saw that the other woman, her friend, was looking in the same direction. And then the tellers stopped what they were doing, and the customers slowly turned, and silence came over the bank. Two men wearing black ski masks and blue business suits were standing to the side of the door. One of them had a pistol pressed against the guard's neck. The guard's eyes were closed, and his lips were moving. The other man had a sawed-off shotgun. "Keep your big mouth shut!" the man with the pistol said, though no one had spoken a word. "One of you tellers hits the alarm, you're all dead meat. Got it?"

The tellers nodded.

"Oh, bravo," Anders said. "*Dead meat.*" He turned to the woman in front of him. "Great script, eh? The stern, brass-knuckled poetry of the dangerous classes."

She looked at him with drowning eyes.

The man with the shotgun pushed the guard to his knees. He handed the shotgun to his partner and yanked the guard's wrists up behind his back and locked them together with a pair of handcuffs. He toppled him onto the floor with a kick between the shoulder blades. Then he took his shotgun back and went over to the security gate at the end of the counter. He was short and heavy and moved with peculiar slowness, even torpor. "Buzz him in," his partner said. The man with the shotgun opened the gate and sauntered along the line of tellers, handing each of them a Hefty bag. When he came to the empty position he looked over at the man with the pistol, who said, "Whose slot is that?"

Anders watched the teller. She put her hand to her

throat and turned to the man she'd been talking to. He nodded. "Mine," she said.

"Then get your ugly ass in gear and fill that bag."

"There you go," Anders said to the woman in front of him. "Justice is done."

"Hey! Bright boy! Did I tell you to talk?"

"No," Anders said.

"Then shut your trap."

"Did you hear that?" Anders said. " 'Bright boy.' Right out of 'The Killers.' "

"Please be quiet," the woman said.

"Hey, you deaf or what?" The man with the pistol walked over to Anders. He poked the weapon into Anders' gut. "You think I'm playing games?"

"No," Anders said, but the barrel tickled like a stiff finger and he had to fight back the titters. He did this by making himself stare into the man's eyes, which were clearly visible behind the holes in the mask: pale blue and rawly red-rimmed. The man's left eyelid kept twitching. He breathed out a piercing, ammoniac smell that shocked Anders more than anything that had happened, and he was beginning to develop a sense of unease when the man prodded him again with the pistol.

"You like me, bright boy?" he said. "You want to suck my dick?"

"No," Anders said.

"Then stop looking at me."

Anders fixed his gaze on the man's shiny wing-tip shoes.

"Not down there. Up there." He stuck the pistol under Anders' chin and pushed it upward until Anders was looking at the ceiling.

Anders had never paid much attention to that part of the bank, a pompous old building with marble floors and counters and pillars, and gilt scrollwork over the tellers' cages. The domed ceiling had been decorated with mythological figures whose fleshy, toga-draped ugliness Anders had taken in at a glance many years earlier and afterward declined to notice. Now he had no choice but to scrutinize the painter's work. It was even worse than he remembered, and all of it executed with the utmost gravity. The artist had a few tricks up his sleeve and used them again and again—a certain rosy blush on the underside of the clouds, a coy backward glance on the faces of the cupids and fauns. The ceiling was crowded with various dramas, but the one that caught Anders' eye was Zeus and Europa—portrayed, in this rendition, as a bull ogling a cow from behind a haystack. To make the cow sexy, the painter had canted her hips suggestively and given her long, droopy eyelashes through which she gazed back at the bull with sultry welcome. The bull wore a smirk and his eyebrows were arched. If there'd been a bubble coming out of his mouth, it would have said, "Hubba hubba."

"What's so funny, bright boy?"

"Nothing."

"You think I'm comical? You think I'm some kind of clown?"

"No."

"You think you can fuck with me?"

"No."

"Fuck with me again, you're history. *Capiche?*"

Anders burst out laughing. He covered his mouth with both hands and said, "I'm sorry, I'm sorry," then snorted helplessly through his fingers and said, "*Capiche*—oh, God, *capiche*," and at that the man with the pistol raised the pistol and shot Anders right in the head.

The bullet smashed Anders' skull and ploughed through his brain and exited behind his right ear, scattering shards of bone into the cerebral cortex, the corpus callosum, back toward the basal ganglia, and down into the thalamus. But before all this occurred, the first appearance of the bullet in the cerebrum set off a crackling chain of ion transports and neuro-transmissions. Because of their peculiar origin these traced a peculiar pattern, flukishly calling to life a summer afternoon some forty years past, and long since lost to memory. After striking the cranium the bullet was moving at 900 feet per second, a pathetically sluggish, glacial pace compared to the synaptic lightning that flashed around it. Once in the brain, that is, the bullet came under the mediation of brain time, which gave Anders plenty of leisure to contemplate the scene that, in a phrase he would have abhorred, "passed before his eyes."

It is worth noting what Anders did not remember, given what he did remember. He did not remember his first lover, Sherry, or what he had most madly loved about her, before it came to irritate him—her unembarrassed carnality, and especially the cordial way she had with his unit, which she called Mr. Mole, as in, "Uh-oh, looks like Mr. Mole wants to play," and, "Let's hide Mr. Mole!" Anders did not remember his wife, whom he had also loved before she exhausted him with her predictability, or his daughter, now a sullen professor of economics at Dartmouth. He did not remember standing just outside his daughter's door as she lectured her bear about his naughtiness and described the truly appalling punishments Paws would receive unless he changed his ways. He did not remember a single line of the hundreds of poems he had committed to memory in his youth so that he could give himself the shivers at will—not "Silent, upon a peak in Darien," or "My God, I heard this day," or "All my pretty ones? Did you say all? O hell-kite! All?" None of these did he remember; not one. Anders did not remember his dying mother saying of his father, "I should have stabbed him in his sleep."

He did not remember Professor Josephs telling his class how Athenian prisoners in Sicily had been released if they could recite Aeschylus, and then reciting Aeschylus himself, right there, in the Greek. Anders did not remember how his eyes had burned at those sounds. He did not remember the surprise of seeing a college classmate's name on the jacket of a novel not long after they graduated, or the respect he had felt after reading the book. He did not remember the pleasure of giving respect.

Nor did Anders remember seeing a woman leap to her death from the building opposite his own just days after his daughter was born. He did not remember shouting, "Lord have mercy!" He did not remember deliberately crashing his father's car into a tree, or having his ribs kicked in by three policemen at an anti-war rally, or waking himself up with laughter. He did not remember when he began to regard the heap of books on his desk with boredom and dread, or when he grew angry at writers for writing them. He did not remember when everything began to remind him of something else.

This is what he remembered. Heat. A baseball field. Yellow grass, the whirr of insects, himself leaning against a tree as the boys of the neighborhood gather for a pickup game. He looks on as the others argue the relative genius of Mantle and Mays. They have been worrying this subject all summer, and it has become tedious to Anders: an oppression, like the heat.

Then the last two boys arrive, Coyle and a cousin of his from Mississippi. Anders has never met Coyle's cousin before and will never see him again. He says hi with the rest but takes no further notice of him until they've chosen sides and someone asks the cousin what position he wants to play. "Shortstop," the boy says. "Short's the best position they is." Anders turns and looks at him. He wants to hear Coyle's cousin repeat what he's just said, but he knows better than to ask. The others will think he's being a jerk, ragging the kid for his grammar. But that isn't it, not at all—it's that Anders is strangely roused, elated, by those final two words, their pure unexpectedness and their music. He takes the field in a trance, repeating them to himself.

The bullet is already in the brain; it won't be outrun forever, or charmed to a halt. In the end it will do its work and leave the troubled skull behind, dragging its comet's tail of memory and hope and talent and love into the marble hall of commerce. That can't be helped. But for now Anders can still make time. Time for the shadows to lengthen on the grass, time for the tethered dog to bark at the flying ball, time for the boy in right field to smack his sweat-blackened mitt and softly chant, *They is, they is, they is.*

RANDOM HOUSE AUDIOBOOKS

Listen to

The Night in Question

by

Tobias Wolff

Read by the Author

Running time: 3 hours, select unabridged stories • 2 cassettes

AT YOUR BOOKSTORE or call TOLL FREE 1-800-726-0600.
*When calling or ordering by mail, please indicate tracking code: 026-93

**Please send me the audiocassette edition (0-679-45567-1) of
The Night in Question by Tobias Wolff.**

_____ @ $18.00	=	_____
(Quantity)		
Shipping/Handling*	=	_____
Subtotal	=	_____
Sales Tax (where applicable)	=	_____
Total Enclosed	=	_____

*Please enclose $4.00 to cover shipping and handling (or $6.00 if total order is more than $30.00).

☐ If you wish to pay by check or money order, please make it payable to Random House Audio Publishing.

☐ To charge your order to a major credit card, please fill in the information below.

Charge to   ☐ American Express   ☐ Visa   ☐ MasterCard

Account No._____ Expiration Date_____

Signature_____

Name_____

Address_____

City_____ State_____ Zip_____

Send your payment with the order form above to:
Random House Audio Publishing, Dept. CC, 25-1, 201 East 50th Street, New York, NY 10022
Prices subject to change without notice. Please allow 4-6 weeks for delivery.

For a complete listing of Random House AudioBooks, write to the address above.